Welcome to the January 2009 collection of Harlequin Presents!

This month be sure to catch the second installment of Lynne Graham's trilogy VIRGIN BRIDES, ARROGANT HUSBANDS with her new book, *The Ruthless Magnate's Virgin Mistress.* Jessica goes from office cleaner to the billionaire boss's mistress in Sharon Kendrick's *Bought for the Sicilian Billionaire's Bed,* and sexual attraction simmers uncontrollably when Tara has to face the ruthless count in *Count Maxime's Virgin* by Susan Stephens. You'll be whisked off to the Mediterranean in Michelle Reid's *The Greek's Forced Bride,* and in Jennie Lucas's *Italian Prince, Wedlocked Wife,* innocent Lucy tries to resist the seductive ways of Prince Maximo. A ruthless tycoon will stop at nothing to bed his convenient wife in Anne McAllister's *Antonides' Forbidden Wife,* and friends become lovers when playboy Alex Richardson needs a bride in Kate Hardy's *Hotly Bedded, Conveniently Wedded.* Plus, in Trish Wylie's *Claimed by the Rogue Billionaire,* attraction reaches the boiling point between Gabe and Ash, but can either of them forget the past?

We'd love to hear what you think about Presents. E-mail us at Presents@hmb.co.uk or join in the discussions at www.iheartpresents.com and www.sensationalromance.blogspot.com, where you'll also find more information about books and authors!

She's his in the bedroom,
but he can't buy her love...

Showered with diamonds, draped in exquisite lingerie, whisked around the world in the lap of luxury...

The ultimate fantasy becomes a reality.

Live the dream with more MISTRESS TO A MILLIONAIRE titles by your favorite authors.

Available only from Harlequin Presents®

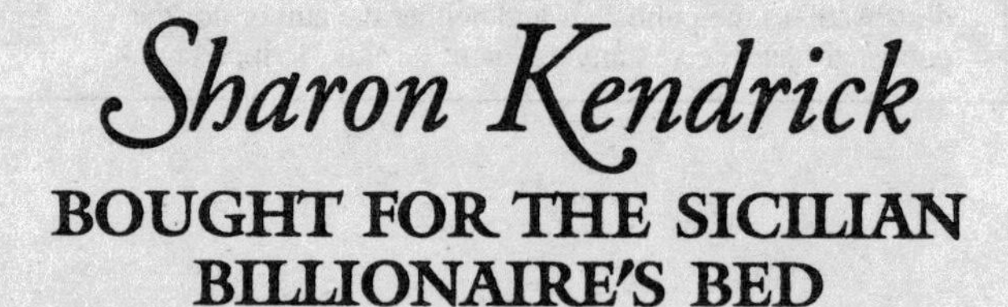

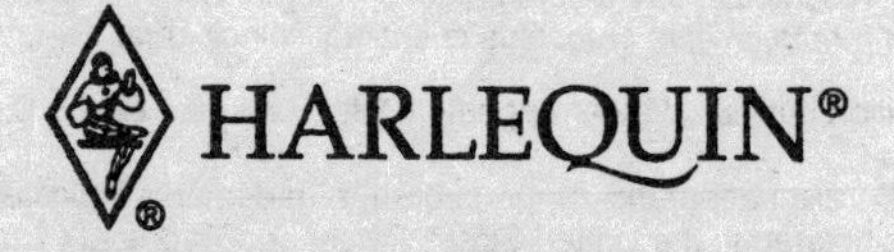

TORONTO • NEW YORK • LONDON
AMSTERDAM • PARIS • SYDNEY • HAMBURG
STOCKHOLM • ATHENS • TOKYO • MILAN • MADRID
PRAGUE • WARSAW • BUDAPEST • AUCKLAND

ISBN-13: 978-0-373-12789-4
ISBN-10: 0-373-12789-8

BOUGHT FOR THE SICILIAN BILLIONAIRE'S BED

First North American Publication 2009.

This edition published by arrangement with Harlequin Books S.A.

www.eHarlequin.com

Printed in U.S.A.

All about the author...
Sharon Kendrick

When I was told off as a child for making up stories, little did I know that one day I'd earn my living by writing them!

To the horror of my parents, I left school at sixteen and did a bewildering variety of jobs: I was a London DJ (in the now-trendy Primrose Hill!), a decorator and a singer. After that I became a cook, a photographer and eventually a nurse. I was a waitress in the south of France and drove an ambulance in Australia. I saw lots of beautiful sights, but could never settle down. Everywhere I went I felt like a square peg—until one day I started writing again, and then everything just fell into place. I felt like Cinderella must have when the glass slipper fit!

Today I have the best job in the world—writing passionate romances for Harlequin Books. I like writing stories that are sexy and fast paced, yet packed full of emotion—stories that readers will identify with, that will make them laugh and cry.

My interests are many and varied—chocolate and music, fresh flowers and bubble baths, films and cooking, and trying to keep my home from looking as if someone's burgled it! Simple pleasures—you can't beat them!

I live in Winchester (one of the most stunning cities in the world—but don't take my word for it, come see for yourself!) and regularly visit London and Paris. Oh, and I love hearing from my readers all over the world...so I think it's over to you!

With warmest wishes,

Sharon Kendrick
www.sharonkendrick.com

To Janet, Barbara and Allen, with love.

CHAPTER ONE

'*MADONNA MIA!*'

The words sounded as bitter as Sicilian lemons and as rich as its wine, but Jessica didn't lift her head from her task. There was a whole floor to wash and the executive cloakroom still to clean before she could go home. And besides, looking at Salvatore was distracting. She swirled her mop over the floor. *Much* too distracting.

'What *is* it with these women?' Salvatore demanded heatedly, and his eyes narrowed when he saw he was getting no response from the shadowy figure in the corner. 'Jessica?'

The question cracked out as sharply as if he had shot it from a gun—taut and harsh and unconditional—and Jessica raised her head to look at the man who had fired it at her, steeling herself against his undeniable attraction, though that was easier said than done.

Even she, with her scant experience of the opposite sex, recognised that men like this were few and far between, something which might account for his arrogance and his famous short temper. Salvatore Cardini—

the figurehead of the powerful Cardini family. Dashing, dominant and the darling of just about every woman in London, if the gossip in the staff-room was to be believed.

'Yes, sir?' she said calmly, though it wasn't easy when he had fixed her within the powerful and intimidating spotlight of his eyes.

'Didn't you realise I was talking to you?'

Jessica put her mop into the bucket of suds and swallowed. 'Er, actually, no, I didn't. I thought you were talking to yourself.'

He glowered at her. 'I do not,' he said icily, in his accented yet flawless English, 'make a habit of talking to myself. I was expressing my anger—and if you had any degree of insight then you might have recognised that.'

And the subtext to *that*, Jessica supposed, was that if she possessed the kind of insight he was talking about, then she wouldn't be doing such a lowly job as cleaning the floor of his office.

But in the past months since the influential owner of Cardini Industries had flown in from his native Sicily, Jessica had wisely learnt to adapt to the great man's quirks of character. If Signor Cardini wished to talk to her, then she would let him talk away to his heart's content. The floor would always get finished when he left for the night. You ignored the head of such a successful company at your peril!

'I'm sorry, sir,' Jessica said serenely. 'Is there something I can help with?'

'I doubt it.' Moodily, Salvatore surveyed the computer screen. 'I am invited to a business dinner tomorrow night.'

'That's nice.'

Turning his dark head away from the screen, he threw her a cool stare. 'No, it is not *nice*,' he mocked. 'Why do you English always describe things as *nice*? It is necessary. It makes good business sense to socialise with these people.'

Jessica looked at him a little helplessly. 'Then I'm afraid I don't really see what the problem is.'

'The problem is—' Salvatore read the email again and his lips curved with disdain '—that the man I'm doing business with has a wife—a rather pushy wife, it would seem. And the wife has friends. Many friends. And…' the words danced on the screen in front of him '"Amy is longing to meet you,"' he read. '"And so are her girlfriends—some of whom have to be seen to be believed! Don't worry, Salvatore—we'll have you engaged to an Englishwoman before the year is out!"'

'Well, what's wrong with that?' asked Jessica shyly, even though a stupidly misplaced pang of jealousy ran through her.

Salvatore gave a snort of derision. 'Why do people love to interfere?' he demanded. 'And why in *Dio's* name do they think that I am in need of a wife?'

Jessica gave a helpless kind of shrug. She didn't think he actually wanted an answer to this particular question and she rather hoped she didn't have to give him one. Because what could she say? That she suspected people were trying to marry him off because he was rich and well connected as well as being outrageously good-looking.

And yet despite the head-turning quality of his looks she thought his face was rather ruthless and cold when you got up close. True, the full mouth was sensual, but it rarely smiled and there was something rather forbidding about the way he could fix you with a gaze which froze you to the spot. Yet somehow, looking the way Salvatore did, he could be forgiven almost anything. And he was.

She'd seen secretaries swoon and tea-ladies get flustered in his presence. She'd observed his powerful colleagues regard him with a certain kind of deferential awe and to allow him to call all the shots. And she'd watched simply because he was a joy to watch.

He was tall and lean and his body was honed and hard, with the white silk shirt he wore hinting at the tantalising shape of the torso beneath. Raven-dark hair contrasted with glowing olive skin and completed the dramatic colour pallet of his Mediterranean allure.

But it was his eyes which were so startling. Bright blue—like the bluest sky or the sea on the most summery day of the year. Jessica had never imagined an Italian having eyes which were any other colour than black. The intensity of their hue seemed to suck all the life from his surroundings and sometimes she felt quite dizzy when they were directed on her. Like now.

And from the faintly impatient crease between his dark brows it seemed that he was expecting some kind of answer to his question.

Distracted by his presence, she struggled to remember exactly what it was he'd asked her. 'Perhaps they think you want a wife because you're...er, well—you're about the right kind of age to get married, sir.'

'You think that?' he demanded.

Jessica felt trapped. Backed into a corner. She shook her head. If he wasn't planning to whisk *her* off her feet, then she thought he should remain a lifelong bachelor!

'Actually, no. Your marital future is not something I've really considered,' she hedged. 'But you know what people are like. Once a man passes thirty—which I assume you have—then everyone starts to expect marriage.'

'*Sì*,' said Salvatore and he ran a slow and thoughtful thumb over the hard line of his jaw where the shadow of new growth had already begun to rasp even though he had shaved that very morning. 'Exactly so. And in my own country it is the same!'

He shook his dark head impatiently. Had he really believed that things would be different here in England? Yes, of course he had. That had been one of his reasons for coming to London—to enjoy a little uncomplicated fun before it came to the inevitable duty of choosing a suitable bride in Sicily. For once in his life he had wanted to escape all the expectations which inevitably accompanied his powerful name—particularly at home.

Sicily was a small island where everyone knew everyone else and the subject of when and whom the oldest Cardini would marry had preoccupied too many, and for too long. On Sicily if he was seen speaking to a woman for more than a moment then her eager parents would be costing up her trousseau and casting covetous eyes over his many properties!

This was the first time he had lived somewhere other than his homeland for any length of time, and it had taken little more than a few weeks to discover that, even within the relative anonymity of England, expectation still ran high when it concerned a single, eligible man. Times changed less than you thought they did, he thought wryly.

Women plotted. And they behaved like vultures when they saw a virile man with a seemingly bottomless bank account. When was the last time he had asked a woman for *her* phone number? He couldn't remember. These days, they all seemed to whip out their cell phones to 'key you in' before he'd even had time to discover their surname! Salvatore had fiercely traditional values about the roles of the sexes, and he made no secret of the fact. And the fact was that men should do the chasing.

'The question is what I do about it,' he mused softly.

Jessica was unsure whether or not to pick up her mop again. Probably not. He was looking at her as if he expected her to say something else and it wasn't easy to know how to respond. She knew exactly what she'd say if it was a girlfriend who was asking her, but when it was your boss, how forthright could you afford to be? 'Well, that depends what choices you have, sir,' she said diplomatically.

Salvatore's long fingers drummed against the polished surface of his desk, the sound mimicking the raindrops which were pattering against the giant windows of his top-floor office suite. 'I always could turn the dinner invitation down,' he said.

'Yes, you could, but you'd need to give a reason,' she said.

'I could claim that I had a cold—how do you say, the "man-flu"?'

Jessica's lips curved into a reluctant smile because the very idea of Salvatore Cardini being helpless and ill was impossible to imagine. She shook her head. 'Then they'll only ask you another time.'

Salvatore nodded. 'That is true,' he conceded. 'Well, then, I could rearrange the dinner so that it was on *my* territory and with *my* guest-list.'

'But wouldn't that be a little rude? To so obviously want to take control of the situation?' she ventured cautiously.

He looked at her thoughtfully. Sometimes she seemed to forget herself—to tell him what she thought instead of what he wanted to hear! Was that because he had grown to confide in her—so that some of the normal rules of hierarchy were occasionally suspended?

He realised that he spoke to Jessica in a way he wouldn't dream of speaking to one of his assistants, or their secretaries—for he had seen the inherent dangers in doing that before.

An assistant or secretary often misjudged a confidence—deciding that it meant he wanted to share a lifetime of confidences with them! Whereas the gulf between himself as chairman and Jessica as cleaner was much too wide for her ever to fall into the trap of thinking something as foolish as that. Yet she often quietly and unwittingly hit on the truth. Like now. He leaned back in his chair and thought about her words.

He had no desire to offend Garth Somerville—nor to appear to snub his wife or her eager friends. And what harm would it do to attend a dinner with such women present? It wouldn't be the first time it had happened, or the last.

Yet he was in no mood for the idle sport of fending off predatory females. Like a child offered nothing but copious amounts of candy, his appetite had become jaded of late. And it didn't seem to matter how beautiful the women in question were. Sex so freely and so openly offered carried with it none of the mystique which most excited him.

'*Sì*,' he agreed softly. 'It would be rude.'

Almost without him noticing, Jessica plucked a cloth and a small plastic bottle from the pocket of her overall and began to polish his desk. 'So it looks like you're stuck with going after all,' she observed, and gave the desk a squirt of lemon liquid.

Salvatore frowned. Not for the first time, he found himself wondering just how old she was—twenty-two? Twenty-three? Why on earth was she cleaning offices for a living? Was she really happy coming in here, night after night, wielding a mop and a bucket and busying herself around him as he finished off his paperwork and signed letters?

He watched her while she worked—not that there was a lot to see. She was a plain little thing and always covered her hair with a tight headscarf, which matched the rather ugly pink overall she wore. The outfit was loose and he had never looked at her as man would automatically look at a woman. Never considered that there might be a body underneath it all, but the movement of her arm rubbing vigorous circles on his desk suddenly drew attention to the fact that the material of her overall was pulling tight across her firm young breasts.

And that there *was* a body beneath it. Indeed, there was the hint of a rather shapely body. Salvatore swallowed. It was the unexpectedness of the observation which hit him and made him a sudden victim to a heavy kick of lust.

'Will you make me some coffee?' he questioned unevenly.

Jessica put her duster down and looked at him and wondered if it had ever occurred to the famously arrogant boss of Cardini Industries that his huge barn of an office didn't just magically clean itself. That the small rings left by the numerous cups of espresso he drank throughout the day needed to be wiped away, and the pens which he always left lying haphazardly around the place had to be gathered up and put together neatly in the pot on his desk.

She met the sapphire ice of his piercing stare without reacting to it. She doubted it. Men like this were used to their lives running seamlessly. To have legions of people unobtrusively working for them, fading away into the background like invisible cogs powering a mighty piece of machinery.

She wondered what he would say if she told him that she was not there to make his coffee. That it wasn't part of her job description. That it was a pretty sexist request and there was nothing stopping him from making his own.

But you didn't tell the chairman of the company that, did you? And, even putting aside his position of power, there was something so arrogant and formidable about him that she didn't quite dare. As if he were used to women running around doing things for him whenever he snapped his fingers and as if those women would rejoice in the opportunity to do so.

She walked over to the coffee machine, which looked as if a small spacecraft had landed in the office, made him a cup and carried it over to his desk.

'Your coffee, sir,' she said.

As she leaned forward he got the sudden drift of the lemon cleaning fluid mixed with some kind of cheap scent and it was an astonishingly potent blend. For a second Salvatore felt it wash unexpectedly over his senses. And suddenly an idea so audacious came to him that for a moment he allowed it to dance across his consciousness.

Imagine if he took someone with him to the dinner party. Someone who might deflect the attention of women on the make. Wouldn't a woman on the arm of a known commitment-phobe send out a loud message to the world that Salvatore Cardini might be taken? Especially if that woman was so unlikely as to take their collective breath away and give them something to gossip about!

The sound of the rain continued to lash against the windows of the penthouse office and Salvatore watched as Jessica picked up her cloth and began to attack a smear of dust. It was as if up until that moment she had been nothing but a piece of paper onto which the outline of a woman had been drawn and only now had the fine detail begun to emerge. Salvatore had an accurate and swiftly assessing eye where women were concerned and for the first time he used it on the woman who was dusting behind a lamp.

Her bottom was curved and her hips were womanly, that was for sure. For the first time he allowed himself to notice the indentation of her waist—and a tiny little waist it was, too.

And yet, although he could be a maverick in business, he liked as many facts as possible at his disposal before he made a decision. He never acted on instinct alone. She might be unsuitable for the task, in so many ways.

'How old are you?' he questioned suddenly, and as she turned round he could see that her eyes were grey and amazingly calm—like the stones you sometimes found at the bottom of a waterfall.

Jessica tried not to show her surprise. It was a very personal question from a man who had always treated her as part of the furniture in the past. Her hand fell from the lamp and the cloth hung limply by her side as she looked at him.

'Me? I'm...I'm twenty-three,' she answered uncertainly.

He stared at her bare fingers. No ring, but these days you could never be sure. 'And you are not married?'

'Married? Me? Good heavens—no, sir.'

'No jealous boyfriend waiting for you at home, then?' he questioned lightly.

'No, sir.' Now why on earth had he wanted to know *that*?

He nodded. It was as he had thought. He gestured to her bucket. 'And you are contented with this kind of work, are you?'

Jessica looked at him from between narrowed eyes. 'Contented? I'm afraid I don't really understand the question, sir.'

He shrugged, gesturing towards her mop and her bucket. 'Don't you? You seem intelligent enough,' he mused. 'I would have thought that a young woman would have had horizons which lay beyond the confines of office cleaning.'

It hurt. Of course it hurt. Apart from being completely patronising he made her sound like some kind of mindless robot in a pinny! Yet surely his damning judgement showed just how arrogant and completely lacking in imagination he was.

Silently, Jessica counted to ten, knowing that several options lay before her. She could pick up her bucket and upend it over that dark head and handsome, mocking face, imagining the water soaking through that fine silk shirt—and his look of dismay and of shock. That would surely be the most satisfying reaction of all. Except, of course, she wouldn't dream of doing it—because that really *would* be professional suicide.

Or she could answer calmly, intelligently and maybe, just maybe, make him eat his judgemental words.

'I'm not a full-time cleaner,' she said.

'You're not?'

'No. Not that there's anything wrong with cleaning,' she defended fiercely as she thought of all her fellow workers at the Top Kleen agency, some of whom squeezed in as many hours as they could while juggling life and work and babies in the most adverse conditions imaginable. 'As it happens, I actually have a day-job. I work for a big sales company and I'm training to be an office manager, but...' Her words tailed off.

'But?' His voice was silken as he prompted her.

She forced herself to confront the dazzling sapphire blaze of his eyes. 'My job isn't particularly well paid. And living in London is expensive. So I top up my salary with a little cleaning work on the side.' Jessica shrugged. 'Lots of people do it.'

Not in his world, they didn't—but didn't her relatively impoverished state make his idea a little less audacious? Maybe they could both do each other a favour.

His eyes flickered over to the rain-splattered window which overlooked the glittering lights of London as he began to wonder what her hair was like underneath that hideous scarf. It might, he thought, be shorn close to her head and coloured in a variety of shades. In which case his suggestion would never be made—for it was inconceivable that Salvatore Cardini would ever be seen out in public with a woman like *that*!

'How do you get home from here?' he questioned idly.

How did he think she got home? By helicopter? 'By bus.'

'You'll get wet.'

She followed the direction of his gaze. Droplets were

scudding down the window and the rain was so thick that you could barely make out the distant buildings beyond. It really was the foulest of nights. 'Looks that way. But that's okay—I'm used to it. Don't they say that rainwater is good for the skin—counteracts all the bad effects of central heating?'

Salvatore ignored the attempt at small talk. 'I'll get my driver to drop you off home. He's waiting outside for me to finish.'

Jessica found herself flushing. 'No, honestly, sir—that's fine. I've got my brolly and a waterproof—'

'Just accept it,' he clipped out. 'What time do you finish?'

'Usually around eight—depends how quickly I work.'

'Make it seven-thirty,' he instructed.

'But—'

'No arguments.' Salvatore glanced at the expensive gold timepiece which gleamed against his wrist and his mouth hardened into an odd kind of smile. 'Consider it done,' he drawled.

And punching out a number on his telephone, he began to speak rapidly in Italian before turning his back on her—as if she was of no real consequence at all.

CHAPTER TWO

JESSICA carried on working at an increased pace in order to get everything done in time, but something had changed and it wasn't just because she was alone in the office with Salvatore. Reserve and shyness had entered her body along with the rapid thunder of her heart as it suddenly occurred to her what she had agreed to. It was like every wistful daydream come true—her gorgeous boss was insisting on giving her a lift home in his chauffeur-driven limo!

And what, Jessica?

You think this is the powerful Sicilian's not-so-subtle attempt to get you, his office cleaner, alone away from the office? Maybe so that he can try to *seduce* you? Yes, sure he is—and he won't really be collecting you in a car at all, but in a glass carriage!

Just accept his generosity with good grace, she told herself as she removed a smear from the coffee machine with a fierce wipe. Enjoy the novelty of a trip home in a luxurious car—it'll make up for all the patronising remarks he made earlier.

At seven thirty on the dot, she picked up her bucket and cleared her throat. 'I'll go and get changed then, sir,' she said, feeling faintly foolish. 'Er, shall I meet you downstairs?'

'Mmm?' Salvatore glanced up at her, his eyes narrowing as if he'd forgotten she was there. 'Yes, sure. Where?'

'Do you know where the back entrance is? It's a bit tricky to find.'

There wasn't a flicker of reaction on his rugged features. 'Not really, but no doubt I can manage without a map,' he said drily. 'The car will be waiting and I don't like to wait. So don't be long.'

'I won't,' said Jessica, and sped off.

But her heart was thundering as she pulled off her pink overall and untied the scarf, wishing that she were wearing something other than a plain skirt and jumper with a great big waterproof coat to put on top.

Yet why should she? This wasn't the kind of job that you dressed up for—dressed down for, more like. She took off her flat black shoes and put them in the locker along with her overall and scarf, then set about brushing her hair—which was her one redeeming feature. It fell to her shoulders and, although it was a rather boring shade of brown, it was good and thick and nearly always shiny.

Jessica squinted into the mirror. Her face looked pale and drained without make-up but she found the end of a tube of lip gloss at the bottom of her handbag and her fingers hovered over it with hesitation.

Would it look a little obvious, as if she might be *expecting* something, if she applied some make-up? But suddenly, Jessica didn't care. A woman had her pride, and even if she happened to be wearing cheap clothes then surely it wasn't a crime to want to make the best of a very bad job.

Fortunately, because she had knocked off slightly early, there was no one else around. None of the other cleaners offering to walk to the bus-stop with her—or, worse, witness her sliding into the back seat of a fancy car.

Why, to any other member of staff it would look… Jessica went pink around the ears. It would look highly suspicious and throw a not very flattering light on her character.

But there was no time for any further doubts. He had specifically told her not to be late, so she grabbed her bag and hurried out. And sure enough there sat a long, low limousine purring like a mighty cat by the back entrance.

Jessica gulped down the dryness in the back of her throat. It was odd to think of someone regarding this kind of car as normal—when in her world it was the type of vehicle which was usually used for weddings.

Convulsively, her fingers clenched around the strap of her handbag. Weddings? *Weddings?* Now what on earth had made that thought pop into her head? Probably because Salvatore had rather surprisingly asked her whether she was married. And why had he wanted to know *that*?

But there was no time for further thought because a uniformed chauffeur was actually opening the door of the luxury car—for *her*!

'Thanks very much,' she said hurriedly, trying to

slide into the back of the car as decorously as possible—something which wasn't especially easy since Salvatore was sitting on the other end of the soft leather seat, his long legs sprawled out in front of him. His arms were crossed and she couldn't make out the expression on his face because the interior of the car was shadowed, but she saw the glint in his narrowed eyes as he watched her.

'So here you are,' he murmured, though his initial thought was one of disappointment. His crazy scheme was just that, he realised. Crazy. With her cheap and bulky coat concealing her slight frame and her pale face she looked just what she was. Ordinary. There was *no way* that this young woman could accompany him to anything, other than perhaps to help carry his shopping in to the apartment. Who would believe that a man like him was dating a woman like her? Nobody with more than one brain cell, that was for sure. 'Where do you live?'

Jessica sat bolt upright. 'Shepherd's Bush.' She gave the name of the road to the driver, who then closed the interconnecting glass so that she was left alone with Salvatore. The last time she had felt as out of place as this was her last day at school, when she'd forgotten that it was a 'no uniform' day.

Salvatore's mouth curved with wry amusement as he registered her stiff frame and uptight body-language. She was nervous, he realised. Did she think that he was about to leap on her? If so, then she clearly had an overinflated view of her own appeal! 'Relax,' he said softly.

Jessica leant back in the seat—though the leather was so soft and squishy that it was hard to believe that she was actually sitting in a car.

'This is really very kind of you,' she said.

'Not a problem.'

'Where...where do *you* live?' It seemed like a very personal question to ask—but what *were* the rules for a situation like this? She couldn't spend an entire journey asking him if he was satisfied with the level of cleanliness in his office!

'Chelsea.'

Of course he did. Rich, glamorous Chelsea with its glorious white villas and springtime trees daubed with cherry blossom.

'I don't want to take you out of your way, sir.'

The 'sir' seemed oddly inappropriate under the circumstances, but she was a thoughtful little thing, he realised. Salvatore smiled as he leaned back and glanced out of the window.

'I can easily have the driver drop me off first if I choose,' he said coolly. 'But there are parts of your city with which I am unfamiliar—and so I shall see this place Shepherd's Bush for myself.'

Don't hold your breath, Jessica wanted to say, but instead she smiled back. She half wondered if she should chat and ask him about whether he was enjoying his time in England, but he seemed to have an aversion to small talk. And besides, he was the kind of man who liked to lead a conversation—not to follow it.

Salvatore felt oddly soothed by the silence which

filled the car and which—surprisingly—she didn't try to fill with inane chatter. Why could women never see the value in peace and always insist on shattering it with unnecessary words?

They drove through a rainy city and for once he felt completely cocooned within the purring warmth of the car. It was all too easy to take luxury for granted, he found himself thinking as the limousine slowed to turn into a road featuring a row of terraced houses.

'It's that one on the end,' said Jessica, glad that the journey had passed without anything going wrong. But she also felt strangely reluctant to leave the sumptuous cosiness in exchange for the cold reality outside. 'Just here.'

'You own this, do you?' questioned Salvatore as the car came to a halt in front of a small house.

Jessica turned to him. Was he crazy? No, he was just rich and the rich were different—everyone knew that. It wasn't his fault that he had no comprehension of how people like her lived their lives. She shook her head. 'Property's hugely expensive in London. I rent—in fact, I share this house with two other girls. Willow works in the fashion business and Freya is an air stewardess—though she's away a lot.'

But Salvatore wasn't really listening. Maybe it was because the rain had finally stopped. Or maybe it was because the moon had appeared from behind the dark curtain of a cloud. It was amazing what a little light could do.

He found himself looking down at her face, at skin

which looked impossibly pure and clean. Her grey eyes were illuminated by that same light and so was the subtle gleam of her mouth. Unexpectedly, she looked all eyes and lips and her pauper-like appearance suddenly crumbled to dust in his memory.

'Are you busy tomorrow night?' he questioned suddenly.

Jessica blinked. 'No. Why?'

'How would you like to accompany me to that dinner I was telling you about?'

'You mean, as your *guest*?' she queried, her voice quivering on the brink of astonishment.

What did she imagine he wanted—that he was taking his own personal cleaner? But at least with Jessica, Salvatore knew that he could be upfront. A girl like her was unlikely to read anything into the situation, but he'd better make it clear.

'Yes, of course,' he said impatiently. 'But what I really want is for you to act like my girlfriend—'

'Your *girlfriend*?' she interrupted, even though everyone knew you should never interrupt your boss but this was so bizarre that the normal rules had gone flying out of the window.

'It's just a little role play,' he murmured. 'Nothing too demanding. Gaze into my eyes a little. Look at me adoringly once in a while. Think you could manage that without too much trouble?' His eyes mocked her with the question because Salvatore knew that there wasn't a woman alive who would find *that* an impossible task. 'Get the predators off my back once and for all, and let them know that if I want a woman, then I'll do the choosing myself.'

'But there must be a million women you could ask!' exclaimed Jessica.

'Oh, at least a million,' he answered, with cool and mocking humour. 'But none of them suitable for all kinds of reasons.' The main one being that they saw him as husband-material, something which this little thing would never be guilty of.

'But won't…?' Jessica bit her lip. Wasn't it more than a bit humiliating to have to ask the next question? But ask it she needed to. 'Won't it be slightly unbelievable…someone like me going out with someone like you?'

'Possibly,' Salvatore conceded, his eye flicking disparagingly over her bulky waterproof. 'If you were dressed like that it might be very difficult indeed.'

'Oddly enough, it didn't occur to me to put on my best party dress for work,' she said, hurt.

'You mean you might have something suitable tucked away?'

For a moment she felt like saying no, she didn't, because surely that would get her off the hook? But somehow she didn't think that Salvatore would let it rest now that he'd made up his mind about this strange assignment. If she said that she *didn't* have anything to wear, then mightn't that look as if she was angling to be given something? Just because she cleaned his office didn't mean that she couldn't scrub up well!

And besides, there was an undeniable part of her which

was thrilled at the thought of accompanying Salvatore Cardini to a party. Didn't life sometimes throw opportunities at you which would be a crime to turn down?

'Of course I've something suitable to wear,' she said proudly, and then a sudden, heady sense of her own power swept over her in a way it had never done before. 'But I haven't said I'll go yet, sir.'

The preposterous statement made him smile, but it made a pulse begin to beat heavily at his temple, too. She would be very foolish indeed if she began to tease him—she was dealing with a man and not a boy. He could bend her to his will with the mere whisper of his fingertip.

Fractionally, he leaned forward, his face closer, his voice soft. 'But I think you will, won't you, Jessica? And while we're at it, I think you should lose the "sir", don't you? In the circumstances it might be a bit of a giveaway.'

He was so close that she could see the moonlight glinting in his sapphire eyes and sense his animal warmth, the tangy scent of soap and raw masculinity. This close he was...Jessica felt her heart give an irregular skip. He was irresistible.

Was she playing with fire?

'Yes, I'll come,' she said, and then stumbled out of the car before either of them could change their minds.

CHAPTER THREE

'YOU'RE going *where* tomorrow night?' demanded Willow in a voice of sheer disbelief.

'Out to dinner,' said Jessica faintly as she took off her bulky jacket. The limousine had just driven away and it was almost as if she needed to repeat the words to herself to believe that they were true. 'With Salvatore Cardini.'

Willow's eyes widened. 'That's *the* Salvatore Cardini? The Italian billionaire playboy who owns that company where you play Mrs Mop in the evenings?'

'That's right.'

'Let's make sure we're talking about the same man here, Jessica. Black-haired, blue-eyed, sex-on-legs but with a mean, dangerous look about him?'

'Well, yes—that just about sums him up.'

Willow brushed a lock of dead-straight blonde hair out of her eye. 'You do realise that he's an international playboy with a reputation as a heartbreaker?'

'I sort of guessed that for myself.'

'And that every glossy magazine worth its salt has

been trying to gain access to do a feature on him? Jessica, what are you *like*?'

Jessica shook his head. 'I didn't know *that*—and I don't care and it's no good you looking at me that way, Willow. I know you work for one of those glossies and I know you'd love an exclusive, but you're not getting it via me. Salvatore is my boss—one of the reasons I have that job is because I'm discreet.'

'But it's a rubbish job!'

'Which means I can pay my bills here!' Jessica retorted, thinking of the steep sum she had to shell out for the tiny boxroom of the three-bedroomed house. But then, unlike Willow and Freya, she wasn't cushioned by the comfort of family money if her finances ran into real trouble.

'Perhaps some time you could tell him that your friend would love to do a sympathetic interview and he could even have say on the final copy? I'd be eternally grateful.' Willow shook her elegant head. 'And he's taking you out,' she said. 'Unbelievable!'

Jessica could understand her incredulity only too well. Her housemate lived up to her name—she was tall, blonde and stylish and legions of men were always attempting to beat their way to her door. Yet not even Willow had managed to attract a man of Salvatore's calibre—and here was mousy little Jessica doing just that.

'It *is* a bit incredible,' she admitted.

'So why has he done it, Jessica?'

Jessica dipped a teabag into a mug of boiling water so that her face was partially hidden. Wouldn't it be humiliating to have to tell the whole truth—that essentially she was being taken out as some kind of deterrent to other women? Wouldn't it be acceptable to allow herself the fantasy, just this once—especially as it was just going to be once?

'I think he just wants company,' she prevaricated.

'Yes, but—'

Jessica turned round as suddenly the reality made her heart sting. 'But what, Willow? You mean what's a rich bloke like him doing with a poor, plain girl like me?'

'No, I didn't—'

'Yes, you did,' interrupted Jessica gloomily. 'And what's more—you're right. Don't you think it was the first thing which occurred to *me*?' She walked back into the sitting room and sat down on the battered sofa, her fingers clutching at her steaming mug of tea. How could she have been naïve enough to think about maintaining a fantasy like this for more than a second? Who would ever believe it?

'These people he's having dinner with are trying to set him up and he's fed up with people trying to marry him off,' she explained. 'So he's taking me as a defiant gesture, in the hope that word gets out and they'll stop trying.' She saw Willow's face and knew that further explanation was indeed necessary. 'And presumably he'd picked me and not someone else more glam because I won't get any false hopes in my head. Because I know my place and I'll just accept the evening for what it is.'

'Is he paying you?' asked Willow sharply.

Jessica put her mug down with a shaking hand, her

cheeks flushing. 'You're making me sound like some kind of…of…hooker!'

Willow shook her head. 'That's not what I meant at all. But it seems to me that you're doing him a pretty big favour—so what's in it for you?'

Jessica bit her lip. Honesty not only made you vulnerable, it also made you weak and in a modern world you needed all the bolstering defences you could get. But suddenly she didn't care. 'I just fancy a glimpse into a different kind of life for a change. I've certainly been on the outside looking in for long enough. The only trouble is whether I can fit in and what I'm going to wear.' She looked up at Willow hopefully. 'I was hoping you might be able to help.'

Willow, who was at least four inches taller and several pounds lighter, smiled. 'Oh, I think I can help. Don't worry, Jessica Martin—we're going to make sure you knock his sizzling Sicilian socks off!'

The next day Jessica skipped lunch so she could leave the office early and spent far too long in the bathroom. She nicked her ankle when she was shaving her legs and her nerves built up as the bathwater grew cold and the sky outside the window darkened.

Under Willow's critical eye, she must have tried on twenty different outfits before finding one that she felt comfortable enough to wear, automatically rejecting anything too tight or too low because she thought that would make her look cheap.

By the time eight o'clock arrived her hands were

shaking with nerves and when the doorbell rang it didn't surprise her when she heard Willow yelling: 'I'll go!'

She sprayed on some perfume, took one final glance in the mirror and went to find her boss, who was standing by their rather tatty velvet sofa talking to Willow. And the moment Jessica looked into the narrowed sapphire eyes she knew that her nerves had been justified. In the office he was distracting enough—but tonight he looked as if he should be carrying a government health warning.

His immaculately cut dinner suit emphasised the long legs and the narrow, sexy hips. He looked expensive, urbane, and so totally out of her league that Jessica's heart began to race and she felt the hot pin-pricking of nerves at her forehead. Suddenly she felt daunted. What the hell was she going to *talk* to him about?

'Hello, Jessica,' he said softly.

'H-hello.'

'You look very…different,' he said slowly.

'Well, that's a relief!' she said quickly and caught Willow's warning glance. If she spent the whole night emphasising the differences between them, then the evening was going to be a disaster. 'Er, thank you,' she amended.

Salvatore watched while she picked up her coat. The fitted black silk dress was a little conservative, it was true, but he liked that—and it accentuated a figure which was really very good. His eyes narrowed. Very good indeed. Her hair was thick and shiny and it swung in a healthy bell around her neck. She looked better than he had anticipated—though she was still light years away from his normal type.

But wasn't it strange how your whole opinion of someone could alter in a single moment? Suddenly he was seeing more than the clear grey eyes and the pure skin—now he found his gaze drawn irresistibly to the way the black silk skated so tantalisingly over her pert bottom. His breath was a little unsteady as he took the coat from her and held it open. 'Here, let me.'

Jessica had grown up in a world where men and women considered themselves equals. No man she knew would ever dream of holding open a door or a coat for her, and as she slid her arms into the garment she thought how stupid it was that such a simple little gesture should be so disarming. Was she imagining the lingering brush of his hands and the corresponding quickening of her heart? Had he *meant* to touch her like that?

'Come on,' he said. 'My car is outside.'

'Bye, Salvatore—nice to meet you,' said Willow, with a megawatt smile. 'Hope to see you again.'

They walked out to the waiting limousine, but as the driver opened the door Jessica looked up at the Sicilian and his face looked shadowed in the moonlight.

'Did you...did you tell them you were bringing someone?'

'I did.'

'And what did they say?'

Shaking his head, he placed his hand at the small of her back and propelled her into the car, suddenly wondering if this was such a good idea after all. Was she too unsophisticated to cope with the evening ahead?

'It doesn't matter what they said,' he said softly as

the car pulled away into the traffic. But then she crossed one leg over another and all he could think about was whether the sheer, dark silk which covered her slender legs was tights, or stockings.

Maybe you'll find out later, taunted a voice inside his head as they drove through the darkened streets, and Salvatore cursed silently and shifted in his seat as unexpected and unwanted desire again began to tug at his senses.

It was just at that point that his phone rang and he pulled it out with a feeling of relief and began to speak.

Jessica stared out of the window as Salvatore spent the entire journey conducting a telephone conversation in rapid Italian, which seemed to magnify her feeling of not belonging. And that feeling only intensified when the car drew up outside an enormous house in Knightsbridge, which looked like something you might see in a film.

'Oh, my goodness—it's *huge*,' she breathed.

He glanced at her. 'It's just a house.'

To him it might be just a house—but to Jessica it was the kind of place for which you'd normally have to pay an admission fee. Inside were uniformed staff who whisked her coat away and someone else who guided them through to the murmuring guests, who all looked up as she followed Salvatore into the glittering room.

She was aware of a blur of names and faces as they were introduced, but Jessica's overwhelming feeling was that the women looked like birds of paradise in their jewels and bright dresses and that she had been a fool to come in black—because wasn't that what all the waitresses were wearing?

Their host and hostess were Garth and Amy and there were two other women called Suzy and Clare—neither of whom seemed to be attached to a rather bloodless-looking man named Steve and a wiry individual with light brown hair who introduced himself as Jeremy. And that was it.

So it really *had* been a set-up, thought Jessica as the redhead named Suzy shimmied over to stand directly in front of Salvatore.

'Hi, Salvatore—do you remember me?' she was asking him, with a coy smile. 'We met in Monte Carlo and I told you that Sicily was my favourite place in the whole world.'

Although she was straining to hear while trying to look as if she weren't, Jessica didn't quite catch Salvatore's response, but she turned away with a sudden pang, telling herself that feeling jealous about her partner certainly wasn't on tonight's agenda.

'Champagne?' questioned Garth, offering her an engraved flute with pale liquid foaming up the sides. 'It's rather a good vintage.'

'Yes, please.' Jessica smiled as if she drank vintage champagne every day of her life. She took a sip and began to chat to Jeremy, who—despite his unlikely appearance—turned out to be something very powerful in the City.

'And what about you?' he questioned. 'Do you work?'

Jessica supposed that this was a world where women *didn't* have to work. 'Oh, yes, I'm…I'm…' Oh, *why* hadn't she prepared something? Jessica looked up to find Salvatore watching her.

'Jessica is training to be an office manager,' said the Sicilian smoothly and she blinked at him in surprise. Had he really remembered that?

'Oh, is that how you two met?' butted in Clare. 'In the *office*?'

Jessica's gaze locked with his. Say what you want to say, those blue eyes seemed to tell her.

'Kind of,' said Jessica, and blushed.

Salvatore hid a smile. Oh, but she was perfect for the role! *Perfetto*. The way the blush of rose crept into her cheeks made her look coy and sweet—as if she were embarrassed about a supposed office romance. So that no one, not even the woman Clare with her heavy eye make-up and brazen cleavage—would have had the guts to interrogate her any further.

'Let's go in to dinner, shall we?' said Amy sharply.

A table was laid up with gleaming crystal and silver and studded with tightly bunched white roses in small vases. As she unshook a giant napkin over her knees Jessica found herself wondering whether she was going to be presented with any unfamiliar foodstuffs which she wouldn't have a clue how to eat, even though Willow had given her a crash course in posh dining while she'd been getting dressed. Oysters and artichokes were apparently the biggest hurdles to clear, but thankfully neither of them made an appearance and so she was able to concentrate on what was being said around the table.

Which was easier said than done. Most of the conversation went right over her head and she noticed that most of the food remained uneaten—though everyone seemed to drink plenty of wine.

She forced herself not to feast her eyes on Salvatore—whose black hair and blue eyes and formidable physique seemed to dominate the entire table. Maybe everyone else was aware of him, too, Jessica thought—because the women certainly didn't seem to be intimidated by the fact that he had brought a partner with him. They flirted with him as if flirting had just been invented.

Did he ever get bored with such a gushing reaction? she wondered suddenly as she turned to talk to the man beside her.

What she knew about banking and takeovers could be written on the back of a postage stamp, but she gently quizzed Jeremy about what he did to relax. It turned out that he was mad about fishing and real enthusiasm entered his voice as he told her about digging for bait.

'Rag worms or lug worms?' she enquired and a silence fell over the table.

Jessica looked up to find Salvatore's gaze on her, the bright blue eyes narrowed in mocking query.

'They're talking about worms—*ugh*!' shuddered Clare theatrically, her breasts pushing against the fine silk of her pink dress as if they were fighting to get out.

'You like to fish, do you, Jessica?' questioned Salvatore softly.

For some stupid reason, colour stole into Jessica's cheeks and she shrugged her shoulders a little awkwardly as she answered him. 'Oh, I did a bit, when I was a child.' In that faraway time when her parents had still been alive and the days had always seemed full of sunshine and games. Her mother would take her down to the riverbank and Jessica would sit solemnly with a hook and line dangling from an old gardening cane.

'Presumably you must have been a tomboy,' observed Suzy.

It was like being in one of those awful nightmares where everyone was staring at you waiting for an answer and you couldn't speak. Except that this wasn't a nightmare and she *could* speak. So stand up for yourself, Jessica, she thought. Don't let this woman intimidate you just because she's crazy about Salvatore.

'I liked climbing trees and fishing and swimming in the river, yes,' she said. 'But I never considered them pastimes which were exclusively for boys—why should they be when they're such fun?'

'Bravo!' said Jeremy softly, and laughed.

She felt on a bit of a high for the rest of the meal, especially when Jeremy offered to take her fishing in Hampshire, where apparently he owned a stretch of the river—and he pressed his card into her hand as she was leaving.

But her exhilaration evaporated the moment the car door closed on her and Salvatore and they were enclosed in their own small, private world.

Slowly, he let his eyes drift over her as if reassessing her potential. 'So I have seen the little English mouse in action,' he murmured.

'What...what's that supposed to mean?'

In the darkness his eyes gleamed. 'Quiet. Unassuming. Then she throws off her overall and becomes the unlikely temptress—'

'Temptress?' echoed Jessica. 'I don't think so.'

'Ah, but you tempted Jeremy—that much was plain,' mused Salvatore silkily. There was a pause. 'And you're tempting me. Right now.'

Too late she sensed the danger in the air and too late she read the sexual intent in his eyes.

It was too late for everything, because Salvatore Cardini had pulled her into his arms and started to kiss her with a passion which took her breath away.

CHAPTER FOUR

FOR a moment Jessica thought that this must be like drowning—when they said your life flashed before you. As Salvatore's lips covered hers she saw the past speed by—with its good and bad, its sadness and joy. But it was as if she had been only a shadow of herself before and his powerful kiss was awakening all her senses.

He tasted of wine and desire and promise and Jessica's lips opened beneath his, her fingers reaching up to clutch at his broad shoulders as if she was afraid that she might collapse. But that was just how it felt—as if a sudden gust of air might blow her clean away.

'Salvatore—' she breathed into his mouth, shockingly aware that it was the first time she had ever used his Christian name, but surely such a situation demanded it.

'Sì?' Groaning, he caught her by the waist, his hands moving beneath her coat to rest proprietorially on the silk of her dress. He slid his palms up to her breasts and cupped them, as if he were examining their weight, before fingering their peaking points through the straining silk.

'Oh!' she gasped, in shock and delight.

He stroked her hips. Her bottom. The curve of her thighs—his hunger for her tempered by a sudden shaft of objectivity. This was crazy, he told himself. This was not what he had intended—not at all. Was that why it suddenly seemed unbearably exciting—because he liked to control a situation and here was one which seemed to have blown up in his face? 'Tell me what you like to do, *cara*,' he whispered. 'Show me what you like.'

She touched her lips to his neck; she couldn't seem to stop herself as her every dark fantasy sprang to life. 'Salvatore…' she whispered again.

Her hand had fluttered down to alight like a butterfly on the tensed muscle of his thigh and his head jerked back as it moved away again. 'I live not far from here,' he bit out. 'Come on—we're going. *Adesso*!'

His hungry words wove themselves into her consciousness as her fingers wove into the silken tangle of his dark hair. Jessica felt as if she had stepped on an escalator which was hurtling her towards a shockingly unexpected pleasure. But even while her body gave itself up to the sensations which were washing over her with such sheer, sweet allure she felt the first unwelcome stir of protest in the back of her mind.

'Salvatore—'

'Mmm?'

His lips were at the base of her neck now, drifting in a tantalising path down towards her breasts. And she held her breath, not wanting to break the moment nor the feeling even as some stubborn resistance reared again its unwanted head. Go away, she told her doubts fiercely—but somehow those doubts refused to die. 'I mustn't—'

'*Sì*, you must.' He smiled against her skin as the tip of his tongue flicked against her skin. 'You want to. You know you do.'

Jessica felt herself slipping under—as if sensual dark waters were lapping over her. Her eyelids fluttered open and all she could see was the ceiling of the luxury car. The *car*! He was seducing her in the back seat of his car! 'You…you…oh, *oh*!'

But, ironically, it was as his hand began to slide its way up her thigh that reality hit her like a sudden spray of ice-water and Jessica tore herself out of his arms, wriggling over to the corner where she surveyed him as if she had found herself alone with an unknown and deadly predator.

Her fingers reached for her neck and she could feel the rapid rise and fall of her breast as she struggled to cope with her ragged breathing.

'What…what on *earth* do you think you're doing?' she breathed.

'You know exactly what I'm doing—I'm going to make love to you.'

Jessica swallowed. 'You are *not*!'

'But you want me to.'

Oh, the arrogance and the assurance which was printed all over that gorgeous face—but even worse was the glaring truth which underpinned his words. She *did* want him—more than she could ever remember wanting anyone, but, oh, at what price? Her dignity? Her *job*? She tugged at the black silk dress which had ridden up round her thighs. 'Maybe for a moment I did—but this certainly wasn't supposed to be part of the plan tonight!'

'No?' he drawled, infuriated now by the sudden, abrupt ending and by the growing feeling of disbelief that a woman should be turning him down. And such a woman as this! 'I wasn't aware that we had drawn up some kind of itinerary for the evening.'

'That's not what I meant and you know it!' she flared.

'No?'

'No!' And suddenly Jessica was angry—not just with herself but with him, too. 'Did you think that I'd jump into bed with you at the drop of a hat?' she demanded.

He wanted to say that it was far more likely to be a drop of her panties, which—unbelievably and infuriatingly—he had yet to see. 'I think you were pretty close to it, Jessica. *Sì.*'

'You think that all you have to do is to whisk me off to a fancy dinner in a chauffeur driven car and I'll be so…so…*grateful* that I'll capitulate to you!'

Salvatore was beginning to grow bored now. 'I hadn't actually given it that much thought,' he told her damningly. 'It wasn't a situation I'd anticipated.'

Stupidly enough, this only added to her anger. So now he was saying that he hadn't even considered he might find her attractive enough to make a pass at her! Was that why he had chosen her—because she was too plain to provide any temptation? Well, thank heavens she had seen sense before it was too late.

Imagine if she'd gone back with him—let him make love to her, and then what? Would he have sent her on her way in the middle of the night—to be taken home by his driver, like a toy he had grown bored with playing with? Or, even worse, being given money for a taxi to conveniently disappear from his bed?

'We are just a man and a woman,' he mused, when still she said nothing. 'And sometimes passion comes along when you are least expecting it. It is the way of these things.'

As he spoke he reached out to brush a stray strand of the thick, shiny hair which had fallen over her face and that one innocent, almost tender gesture was almost Jessica's undoing. Because that was the kind of thing that a real lover might do—especially if he was trying hard to seduce you. Not that Jessica was the world's biggest expert on lovers, but she knew what was considered acceptable by most women with a degree of self-respect and what was not.

If she allowed Salvatore to make love to her now, then it would be tantamount to telling him to treat her like a disposable cloth—to be thrown away when he'd finished with her!

And by tomorrow, his desire would have died. Why, he might even thank her for having been level-headed enough to put a stop to things before they got out of hand. True, facing him again in the workplace wasn't going to be the most comfortable option, but there were ways of dealing with that.

She pulled her head back from the enticement of that touch. 'Maybe it's the way of things in the world *you* live in,' she said pointedly. 'But not in mine.'

He searched her face for a teasing look, the telltale expression on her face which would indicate that this was merely female playfulness, but to Salvatore's disbelief there was none. Just the kind of jutting-chinned certainty which women often assumed when they meant something, and which made his heart sink.

This was worse than being back in Sicily! Did she really imagine that he was going to start courting her? That she would allow him certain privileges each night? One night the kiss, the next the breasts—until she breathlessly allowed him to take her whole body, as she would have been hungering for from the very beginning?

Did she really think he had the time or the inclination to waste on a leisurely pursuit of a woman for whom his desire was already waning—someone who should have been *thanking her lucky stars* to be here with him in the first place? His mouth twisted. What a little fool she was—to have called time on what would have been the best experience of her life!

'If you think that such resistance will elevate you to a truly irresistible status in my eyes, then I am afraid you are sadly mistaken, *cara*. Do you not think that I have been privy to every devious game played by women? I know them all—and it won't work, for I am immune to them all.'

Jessica sat bolt upright. She hadn't been so angry since...well, actually, she couldn't *ever* remember being as angry as *this*!

'Oh, don't worry, Signor Cardini,' she retorted, trying to match his withering tone with one of her own and in that hot moment of fury not caring that she might be jeopardising her job. 'I really hadn't given any thought to game-playing—why would I? I thought I was coming out to act as some kind of decoy—not to be leapt on in the back of your car! And now, if you don't mind—I'd like to be taken home.'

There was a moment of brief, stunned silence as the impact of her words sank in, until in the shadowed gloom Salvatore's mouth curved into a cruel and mocking smile. 'I think you forget yourself, *cara mia*,' he drawled damningly. 'You will certainly be dropped off—but only after the car has taken me home.'

He pressed a button by his seat, tersely issued the instruction to his driver and drew a sheaf of documents from one of the side-pockets. And then, clicking on a reading light, he leaned back in his seat and began to flick through them, as if he had simply forgotten she was there.

CHAPTER FIVE

BUT the craziest thing of all was that Salvatore couldn't get Jessica out of his mind—and the irony of this didn't escape him. How could one short, bogus date have resulted in him thinking almost non-stop about his damned cleaner? Unable to shake from his mind the memory of her grey eyes, that pure skin and the decadent delight of those luscious breasts.

The light glinted on his razor as he stared in the mirror, his dark jaw half shaved and his blue eyes narrowed. Intellectually he recognised that her improbable attraction was *because* she had turned him down. He was used to women fawning. Plotting. Enticing and scheming. Why, it was not unknown for a woman to *beg* him to make love to her!

Jessica intrigued him because in a world where one thing was predictable—his effect on the opposite sex—the unexpected would always have the power to tantalise him.

So had she been playing games with him? Knowing that precisely the right button to press was not to let him press any buttons at all? To let him touch a little, but not too much. To give him a taste to whet his appetite but leave him hungering for more?

He went to his club and swam for an hour, had a breakfast meeting in a chandelier-lit room overlooking Hyde Park and took a conference call from an Australian banker before most of the world was awake. Yet still he was restless.

How could some plain and mousy little cleaner know how to handle any kind of man—but especially a man like *him*?

All day long he was distracted, though he was astute enough not to make any major decisions until her infernal perfume had left his senses. Some scent he was unfamiliar with—which had reminded him of springtime and softness and clung to his skin last night until he had viciously washed it off beneath the jets of a cold shower.

'*Maledizione*!' Damn her!

Giovanni Amato—an old friend from Sicily—was flying in from New York and Salvatore had arranged to meet him for dinner. Yet he found himself strangely relieved when Giovanni's secretary rang to say his flight had been delayed, and that he was running late.

'Get him to call me,' Salvatore said to her. 'We'll change it to another night.'

As he slowly put the phone down Salvatore felt the stealthy beat of excitement combined with the strong tang of self-contempt. Surely you aren't hanging around the office waiting to see whether that pale little nobody will dare show her face here tonight? he asked himself furiously.

But as he cleared his desk of paperwork he recognised that maybe he was. He glanced at his watch. That was if she was going to bother to turn up.

He had signed the last of a pile of letters and was just putting his gold pen down on the blotter when he heard the door click open behind him. Salvatore felt himself tense, though he didn't move. He didn't dare move. He hadn't felt this kind of hot, instant lust for a woman for a long time and he wanted to prolong it—knowing that the second he turned round, his fantasy would crumble into dust. He would no longer be looking at the woman who had made him feel so deliciously hard all night, but at some mousey little office worker.

He swivelled the chair round to face her. 'Hello, Jessica,' he said softly.

Clutching her bucket and her mop, Jessica froze as she stared across the huge office in horror.

He was still here!

Despite her leaving his office until the last possible moment—until she was certain that he had gone—Salvatore Cardini was still at his desk, his icy blue eyes mocking her with memories of what had almost happened in his car last night! She bit down on her lip so hard that she risked cutting it and the hand which wasn't holding onto the mop clenched into a tight fist by the side of her pink overall. Of all the nightmare situations, this had to be the very worst.

Hadn't she hesitated about coming in here at all, tempted to phone Top Kleen and tell them she was sick?

And hadn't there been a tiny part of her which had wondered about leaving the agency altogether—to sign on with someone new? Someone who might not have a prestigious client like Cardini, but who would guarantee a peaceful working environment where she would be untroubled by ridiculous fantasies.

But Jessica had a strong work ethic, which made her baulk at such behaviour, as well as a stubborn streak of pride which insisted that she had done nothing wrong. Nothing to be ashamed of.

So where was that strong conviction now? Staring across the vast space, she could see the sardonic glint in Salvatore's eyes. Her mouth as dry as parchment, she drank him in. His black hair, his broad shoulders and outline of that amazing hard body. The image of that same body pressing itself close into hers in the back seat of his car drifted tantalisingly into her mind and fiercely she tried to block it.

What the hell was she going to say to him when their last meeting had ended in a frozen silence?

Just act normally. As if nothing happened. Wipe it from your memory—as he has probably wiped it from his.

She cleared her throat. 'Good evening…' she hesitated. '…sir.'

Salvatore gave a slow, mocking smile. So they were back to 'sir', were they?

His eyes flicked over her. She was wearing the same pink overall which she always wore and her hair was almost completely concealed by the hideous pink scarf. Her face was bare of make-up and her grey eyes were wary, watchful. She looked exactly the same as she always did and yet something had changed.

In him?

Was it because he had kissed those bare lips and tangled his fingers in the glossy hair which now lay covered from his gaze that made him so acutely aware of her presence in a way he had never been before? Was it because he now knew the luscious curves and unexpected temptations of the body which lay beneath the unflattering garment?

'Sleep well?' he questioned softly.

Infuriatingly, Jessica blushed. No, of course she hadn't slept well! She'd spent the entire night tossing and turning and bashing her pillow into shape and then getting up to make herself a cup of camomile tea, unable to get Salvatore out of her mind.

It had been the memory of his kiss which had troubled her more than anything. Because wasn't it rather shaming that in all her twenty-three years—the one kiss which had sent her heart soaring was delivered by a man for whom she'd been nothing but a convenience?

She wondered if he was astute enough to notice how awful she looked. Wouldn't the dark circles beneath her eyes show her to be lying if she claimed to have slumbered like a baby?

'Not really, no,' she answered briskly.

'Me neither. I tossed and I turned all night.' His lips lingered on the words as he leaned back in his chair and studied her. 'But I guess that isn't really surprising, is it, *cara*?'

She wished he wouldn't dip his voice like that—as

if he were dipping a rich, ripe strawberry into a bowl of thick, melted chocolate. And she wished he wouldn't stare at her like that, either. As if it were his unalienable right to arrogantly appraise her, with the kind of slow scrutiny of a man performing an imaginary striptease. So just blank all his sensual allusions. Behave as you normally would and sooner or later he'll tire of the game and leave you alone.

'No, not surprising at all,' she said, deliberately misunderstanding. She picked up a plastic bottle which appeared to show two lemons going into battle against an army of germs. 'The food at dinner was very rich.'

'But you hardly touched a thing all evening,' he reminded her.

'I'm amazed you noticed,' said Jessica.

'Oh, I noticed all right.' His blue eyes gleamed with provocation. 'Just as I noticed that Jeremy Kingston seemed to think you were the most fascinating thing to come into his life since his last tax break.'

'Only because I asked him about fishing. He says he gets fed up with people always wanting to know which bank he's taking over next.'

'Are you aware that he's one of the most powerful financiers in Europe?' questioned Salvatore coolly.

'No, of course I'm not,' scoffed Jessica. 'Finance not only doesn't interest me—it also confuses the life out of me. Now, do you mind if I start working?'

He linked his long fingers together. 'You don't usually ask.'

She wasn't usually remembering just what it felt like

to have his lips all over her neck, his hands splayed over her silk-covered thighs. 'So I don't,' she agreed tightly. 'But under the circumstances, I thought I'd make an exception.'

Clutching her bucket, she walked across the office to the cloakroom, horribly and yet skin-tingling, aware that he was watching every step as she passed him, like a clever cat before it leapt onto a helpless little mouse. She reached for the tap. Hadn't he called her a mouse last night? And wasn't that an insult?

Salvatore could hear the sound of running water and he screwed his eyes together. He had been expecting—what? That she would have prettied herself up for him this evening? Flirted a little? Undone a few buttons and flaunted a little cleavage? Or acted in that deliberately coy way that women sometimes did, and which men could rarely resist, even when they knew they were being manipulated.

Yet here she was, behaving as if nothing had happened!

But nothing *did* happen, his aching body reminded him, and his natural sexual arrogance made his fists clench with anger that frustration imposed on him from such an unlikely source. Noiselessly, he rose from his desk and followed her into the cloakroom. 'You don't usually run away from me either, do you, Jessica?'

She turned round, her face flushed, heart-thumpingly aware of his proximity and the way that he seemed to dominate the space around them. Suddenly, her bravado seemed to have deserted her. 'No, I don't,' she agreed unsteadily.

'Just like you don't usually stare at me all wide-eyed like that, as if I'm the big, bad wolf.'

Jessica attempted to make her face look normal—but how the hell did you do something like that when all you could think of was how utterly irresistible the man was? 'Don't I?'

He smiled, but it was a hard edged smile. 'You know you don't.'

He seemed to be deliberately misinterpreting the situation. Didn't he have any inkling how difficult she was finding this? Didn't he realise that she had feelings for him but was sensible enough to know that such feelings were totally inappropriate? Jessica frowned, but part of her felt a sudden sadness, too.

Usually they had an easy rapport, which sometimes happened when two people of completely different social standing came together. You sometimes heard about very rich men confiding in their driver, or a billionairess divulging all her secrets to the girl who painted her toenails. But it didn't *mean* anything—not in the grand scheme of things.

Because such unlikely relationships only worked on the basis that both parties knew their place. That there were strict boundaries which neither should attempt to cross.

And so it had been with her and Salvatore—until last night. Last night they had broken the rules, big time. The taking her to dinner could have been classified as nothing but a minor transgression—but what had happened afterwards could not.

She couldn't deny what she'd done—or nearly done.

And although she had called a halt to that blissful bout of passion she couldn't deny that her body had been crying out for him.

She looked at him. If she allowed herself to sink further into stupid fantasy, then her body could very easily start crying out for him right now. His black hair was ruffled, the bright blue eyes narrowed and the hard and autocratic line of his jaw was shadowed with new growth. He looked imposing and almost magisterial and a whole universe away from her. Standing here now, it seemed almost impossible to believe that they had briefly been so intimate.

Jessica knew that she had a choice—and the only sane one which lay open to her was not to rise to his teasing remarks or the sensual light which lurked in the depths of his sapphire eyes. He's only playing with you, she told herself, and she knew she couldn't afford to join in—neither financially, nor emotionally. That if she wanted to keep her job and carry on as before, then she had to forget the rapport they used to share. Forget everything except doing what she was paid to do, which was to clean his office.

'I'd better get on with the floor,' she said awkwardly, turning the hot tap on full and then jumping back as the red-hot water splashed onto her hand, and she gave a little yelp of pain. 'Ouch!'

'Sollecita!' Salvatore made a clicking noise with his tongue as he walked over to her. 'Here.' And he calmly turned on the cold tap and held her flaming fingers beneath it.

The water was deliciously cool and soothing but his touch was even more unsettling than the stinging pain. Jessica tried to pull away but he wouldn't let her.

'Leave it under the running water,' he ordered. 'I said, *leave* it, Jessica.'

She didn't have the strength or the inclination to disobey him and yet this was just too odd. He was here, in the most inappropriate of settings, administering hasty first aid to her. She felt dizzy with shock and pleasure. Everything was all wrong and yet through all the confusion of her thoughts came the overwhelming sensation that she liked him touching her.

She swallowed. Of course she liked him touching her—who wouldn't?

After a couple of minutes, he turned the hand over and examined it, tracing a light fingertip over the still-heated flesh. 'I think you'll live,' he said softly.

The surprising gentleness of the contact was completely disarming, as was the sudden deepening of his voice.

'It's okay. I mean, I'm okay,' she amended, trying to pull her hand away.

'Maybe you are,' he objected as he drew her towards the warmth of his body. 'But I'm not.'

Her eyes opened wide, startled by pleasure and shock. 'What…what are you doing?'

'This,' he said, his voice distorting savagely as he stared down into her pale face. 'I have to do this.'

She knew he was going to kiss her—she could read it in the fractional dilation of his eyes. She could sense it in the sudden tension in his body and in the raw tang of masculine desire which made her forget everything she had vowed last night as she'd listened to the ticking of her bedside clock and waited for the alarm to ring. He was going to kiss her and, although she knew she should stop it, she could no more have stopped it than willed the earth to stop turning.

'Salvatore…' she whispered.

The 'sir' had gone once more, he thought, with grim satisfaction. '*Sì*,' he agreed arrogantly, her breath warm against his lips. 'That is my name.'

With a groan, he drove his mouth down on hers. She tasted sweet and minty, as if she had just brushed her teeth. Had she done that specially, hoping that he would kiss her? The thought that she had been anticipating this—wanting this—made him harder still.

He pulled her closer, his hands reaching down to cup her buttocks, and for the first time he appreciated how small she was. Positively tiny. In the car their bodies had been on a level, but now she seemed to slip into his arms and disappear into them, melding into his body like a pocket Venus.

Jessica clutched onto his shirt as his lips beguiled her, the palms of his hands skating with arrogant possession over her bottom. On and on his mouth continued to plunder hers until suddenly her knees threatened to give way—and perhaps he also sensed too that things were getting out of hand because he stopped kissing her, though he didn't let her go. She gazed up at him uncertainly, in a daze.

His blue eyes looked almost black and his breathing was ragged and there was an odd kind of expression on his face, as though he liked what he was doing but despised it all at the same time.

'We can't stay here,' he said flatly. 'Come back to my apartment.'

Jessica swallowed. Stay focussed. Don't behave like you're expendable. You may have a lowly job but that doesn't mean you don't have pride. 'No,' she answered stubbornly. 'I can't.'

He shook his head impatiently. 'Forget the cleaning for tonight.'

Jessica almost laughed. He thought that her refusal was solely about some loyalty to the dust levels in his office! Was that the only kind of thought he believed her capable of? 'That wasn't what I meant.'

Salvatore stilled as he heard the note of determination which had crept into her voice. He had allowed her a token show of defiance last night—but she was trying his patience now. Was she daring to *bargain* with him?

'What *did* you mean?' he demanded dangerously.

But Jessica was not going to be bowed or bullied simply because he was in a position of authority. She lifted her chin up and stared at him. 'You think I'm just going to come back with you to your flat and let you make love to me?'

'Why, are you planning to go all demure on me when we both know that's what you want, *cara mia*?'

Jessica took a step back, needing the space and looking at him with a kind of defiance. 'Life isn't just about doing what you want, Salvatore, it's about doing what's right, too.'

Dark eyebrows rose in haughty surprise. 'Don't tell me we're going to start talking morals now?'

Jessica shook her head, hurt now, but impatient, too. 'Is it because I clean your offices that you think you can just pick me up like an ornament and put me down again? Do you treat all women like that? No, of course you don't! If I were someone else—you'd at least do me the courtesy of going through the motions of normal behaviour. You might ask me out to the theatre, or take me out to dinner. You might at least *pretend* that you're interested in getting to know me as a person, rather than how quickly you can get me into your bed!'

Her breathing was all over the place and she stared at him with a boldness he had rarely seen directed at him, and certainly never by a woman.

'Finished?' he questioned.

Go on, then, thought Jessica. Sack me, and see if I care! 'Yes,' she said.

Salvatore's lips twisted into an odd kind of smile. 'I think I get the drift. You're objecting not because I want to go to bed with you, but because I have not gone through the necessary rituals which society demands?'

'Are you making fun of me?'

'Not at all. For who am I to argue in the face of such a passionately put plea?' Such passion boded well for the bedroom, he mused as he looked down at her flushed cheeks with some amusement. 'What is it they say? The mouse who roared. Very well—I have heard you, my little mouse, and we shall play the games according to your rules.' He glimmered her a mocking look. 'So will you have dinner with me, Jessica?'

She swallowed. 'As another pretend date, you mean?'

He shook his head and this time his tone was almost gentle. 'No. As a real one this time.'

She was so taken aback that for a moment words completely failed her. 'When?'

He gave a low laugh. 'How about Tuesday?'

Jessica stared at him. How could he go from such urgency to a day which seemed ages away? 'Tuesday?' she questioned tentatively.

'*Sì*, that is the first evening I have free. I'm flying to Rome for the weekend.'

'*Rome*?'

'Mmm. Ever been there?'

'No. Never.' She wanted to ask him who he was going to Rome with, but that was none of her business.

He moved a little closer and he could see the sudden wild darkening of her eyes, the instinctive way that her lips parted. He should kiss her now, take her here and have done with it—it wouldn't be hard to overcome her coy reluctance.

Yet he had never been forced to wait. Nor to dance attention to a woman's demands, and it was oddly exciting. Why not let her enjoy her brief moment of power while it lasted? Soon he would have her exactly where he wanted her. 'So are you going to see me on Tuesday?' he murmured.

'Yes, I can do Tuesday,' she whispered.

He stared down at her for one long moment, drifting a contemplative finger over the outline of her lips and feeling them tremble beneath his touch. He read her silent plea to have him kiss her once more, to seal the agreement in another traditional way—and with a brief, hard smile he turned away. Let her simmer. Let her wait as she had forced him to wait.

'Until then, *cara*,' he said softly.

And holding onto her stinging hand, Jessica was left weakly staring after him as he walked out of the room without another word.

CHAPTER SIX

THE restaurant took Jessica's breath away. She'd heard of it, of course—but never actually imagined eating there. It was right in the middle of London's theatreland and so anonymous from the outside that you wouldn't know it was there. A secret door opened straight onto the pavement. You stepped in from a crowded and busy street and it was like entering a different world.

It was a large yet intimate space with stained glass windows filtering in coloured light while keeping it private from prying eyes outside. Although it was a Tuesday evening, it was packed out. One of those places where it was impossible for mere mortals to get a table at short notice, though Salvatore had managed it without any trouble.

He seemed to be known here, thought Jessica as they were shown to their table. The waiters beamed. The sommelier nodded at him with a smile. Were staff in places like this taught to remember the names of all their influential customers, she wondered—or was it Salvatore's bright blue eyes and dark, towering presence which would always stamp him indelibly on people's minds?

She had never felt more self-conscious as they wove their way through the linen-draped tables. She saw a couple of faces she recognised from TV and spotted a well-known author who had won a literary prize last year and whose book she had at home.

The women all looked very thin and very beautiful. A couple of them glanced up as they passed and Jessica was certain she wasn't imagining their faint frowns. They looked as if they were trying—and failing—to place her.

What's a guy like him doing with a girl like her? their carefully made-up eyes seemed to ask—or was that just her own insecurity talking? All the same, she wondered what they'd think if they knew the truth!

'You are amused by something?' questioned Salvatore as she sat down.

Jessica let the waiter unfold a giant napkin onto her lap. 'I'm just hoping I don't pick up the wrong fork.'

Salvatore gave a low laugh. 'I remember the first time I left Sicily. I went to stay in France and one of my uncles took me out to eat in the most famous restaurant in Paris. I could see what looked like fifty pieces of cutlery at each setting, and the very *crème* of Parisian high society surrounding me.'

'And were you scared?' asked Jessica, for a moment forgetting all her nerves, the anxieties which had plagued her all day, about how the evening was going to end and whether she looked okay.

Salvatore shrugged. He supposed that it wouldn't be

particularly helpful to her to know that nothing ever really scared him. That men were there to be strong and doubts were for women—but he wasn't going to invent a timid persona just to make her feel better.

'No. I watched my uncle and copied exactly what he did. The only difference was that he left food on his plate. It was a thing that people did then, to show that they were not peasants, but I had the hunger of youth, and finished mine. Every scrap.'

Jessica nodded, eager to hear more. The unexpected glimpse into his past made him seem less daunting somehow. More like the man who usually chatted to her in the office before this whole sexual attraction thing had blown up in their faces. It made it easier to forget what this evening was about and to pretend that they were alone in this gorgeous restaurant for no other reason than that they liked one another.

'And don't tell me,' she teased, 'that no food has ever tasted as good as the meal you ate that night?'

He shook his dark head. 'On the contrary,' he demurred softly. 'They had messed around with the menu so that everything I ate was almost unrecognisable as the original ingredient. The best food of all is simple, and fresh—the fresher the better. The fish you pull from the water yourself and throw onto the flames. The rabbit whose blood is still warm and which goes straight into the pot. And no orange is sweeter than the one plucked from the tree.' But other appetites had been satisfied that night, he recalled, with an ache of nostalgia.

He remembered the beautiful waitress who had

slipped him her phone number while his uncle was paying the bill. Later, he remembered sneaking out to her tiny room close to the *Sacre Coeur* and the long, sensual night which had followed. The sound of the church bell striking the hour and voices shouting in the street outside as she had moaned her pleasure beneath him. The bowl of strong, sweet coffee he had drunk amid the rumpled sheets in the morning. How sharpened his senses had been then.

He stared at Jessica, at the way her hair hung in two shiny wings by the side of her face, and he felt an unexpectedly savage kick of lust. He wanted her, he realised, with a sharp hunger he had not felt in a long time.

All weekend he had thought about just how much he wanted her and how her sweet, flowering perfume had invaded his senses. He felt a pulse beating deep at his groin. Maybe he just liked the kind of woman who would never make any demands on him.

The waiter came over with two glasses of champagne and made as if to leave them alone with their menus, but Salvatore waved him back, eager for the formality and constraints of the meal to be over. 'Shall we order?' he questioned unevenly.

'Yes, of course.' He might as well have announced, Let's get it over with! Jessica knew exactly why he wanted to speed through the meal—she could read it in the way he was looking at her and the sudden tension in the air. The way his face had changed. The sudden tension in his body.

This whole occasion was a formality, she reminded

herself painfully—it wasn't real, it was phoney. And suddenly the nerves which had been simmering away came bubbling up to the surface. She forced a smile, clasping her hands together so he couldn't see them trembling. 'What would you recommend?'

'Let's have steak, and salad, oh, and a half bottle of Barolo,' he added, glancing up at the waiter and then leaning back in his chair to study her once the man had gone. 'So where do you usually go to eat?' he questioned politely.

'Small independents, mainly,' she answered, horribly aware that they were now going through the motions of having a conversation. As if Salvatore really cared where she normally ate! 'Though it's hard when there are so many chains. I'm not really mad about—'

'You're looking very…delectable tonight,' he cut in softly.

'Am I?'

'Yes, you are. Almost unrecognisable. That colour suits you.'

'Thank you.' Nervously, Jessica licked her bottom lip as she responded to a compliment she wasn't really sure she merited. It was another borrowed outfit, loaned once again by Willow, but given more grudgingly this time.

'He's taking you out *again*?' Willow had demanded in disbelief when Jessica had arrived back from work, pale-faced with shock as she'd shared her news.

'That's right. For dinner.'

She hadn't said why. She hadn't dared. She found it hard to believe it herself—that she should be pursuing something which had the power to wreck her admittedly dull, but relatively ordered life. *She* had been the one who had wanted this evening to happen and yet now it had arrived she felt as flat as a punctured balloon.

And that was the trouble. When Salvatore had taken her to that dinner party she'd had nothing to lose—she had been there acting as his girlfriend. She had been given a role and known how to play it. But tonight was different. The meal was one that *she* had demanded in order to put a gloss of respectability over something which wasn't respectable at all. She was contemplating going to bed with her boss.

Tonight she was here as herself and never had the differences between them seemed so glaringly obvious. Had she really thought that they could just sit through a meal together and then go off to have sex as if it were the most natural thing in the world? Didn't matter how much she wanted him or how long she'd had a stupid crush on him—deep down she knew this was wrong. It had to be wrong, surely, when two people came from such different worlds?

Jessica stared down at her plate. 'It was a mistake to come here tonight,' she said unhappily.

Salvatore surveyed the gleaming and neatly parted crown of her head, the way that her silk-covered shoulders were hunched in an expression of defeat. 'Why do you say that?'

'Because…oh, come on, Salvatore—you *know* why,' she whispered.

'I thought you wanted to eat dinner with me.'

'Yes, I did—but maybe I was wrong to want it. Or maybe the circumstances surrounding it were wrong. Are wrong.'

'You weren't being so coy or so dismissive the other day,' he said slowly.

'I know that. And maybe I'm regretting it now.'

'Are you?' When she didn't answer, his voice deepened into a silken caress. 'Jessica, look at me.'

In the background she could hear the distant laughter and chatter of the other diners and the chink of glass and cutlery. Everything sounded as if it were coming from a long way away.

Reluctantly, she raised her head and stared into the bright blue eyes—instantly caught and mesmerised by their sensual light. She could feel the inevitable leaping of her heart, the heavy singing of excitement in her blood as she looked across the table into his ruggedly handsome face.

Had he known that would happen—one look and she would be captivated? Yes, of course he had. He wasn't a stupid man and he must have capitalised on his undeniable power over women time and time again.

Reaching across the table, he took one of her hands in his, turning it over to study it. The nails were cut short and filed down sensibly and the skin was unusually dry. The women he usually dated had silky-soft flesh, buffed and creamed and indulged during their innumerable sessions at the beauty salon.

These were worker's hands, he realised with a start, and suddenly he found himself wanting to pamper her.

He had thought that this place might be a treat for her—but now he could see that it might be something of an ordeal. 'We don't have to stay here, you know,' he said.

'But we've only just ordered.'

'We can cancel it. Go back to my place and have something there, if you're hungry.'

'I'm not.'

'No.' Their eyes met. 'Neither am I.'

Jessica swallowed, because now his thumb was stroking a tantalising little circle on her palm. He was weakening a resolve which was already terminally weak. She looked at the sensual curve of his lips, scarcely able to believe that they had kissed her so passionately, and yet just the touch of him was making her shiveringly aware that they had. 'Won't it look…strange if we just walk out?'

Salvatore smiled. 'Who cares what it looks like? I don't spend my life seeking the opinion of others.' He gave a shrug and his thumb began to stroke a bigger circle, and then to trace a slow path up the length of her middle finger. He smiled as he saw her eyes darken at the unconscious eroticism. 'Come on,' he ordered huskily.

In a way, it was the craziest solution of all. If Jessica had felt out of place before, then choosing to leave just as the waiter was bringing out the red wine and salad was guaranteed to focus attention on them.

But even in spite of that, she felt an overwhelming sense of relief that they were going—because anything was better than trying to maintain a façade that this was like a normal date, when clearly it was anything but. Of having to try to chew her way through a piece of steak, no matter how tender it was, when food was the last thing she wanted right now.

When they got outside she could tell him that the whole thing had been a bad idea and that it had all been a stupid mistake on her part. She should never have asked for this. But at least if she called a halt to it now, she wouldn't get hurt.

The January air which hit them was bitingly cold and Jessica wished she'd remembered to bring gloves.

'I think maybe it's best if we just forget all about tonight,' she said, pulling her coat tighter around her. 'I can make my own way home on the Tube.'

His eyes narrowed. 'Are you crazy?' he questioned silkily. 'You think I'm letting you go anywhere without me tonight?' The limousine purred up to a silent halt beside them and, aware of the paparazzi hanging around, he pulled open the door and quickly pushed her inside.

'Salvatore,' she said as he slid onto the back seat beside her and Jessica's heart began to race. 'You can't take me somewhere against my will.'

'Does protesting and playing the innocent salve your conscience?' he questioned. 'Or does it simply turn you on?'

'That's unfair. And it's not true.'

'No?'

She shook her head. 'No.'

He tipped her pale face upwards, his thumb beneath her chin. Her grey eyes were smokier tonight, he thought, and her lips gleamed at him enticingly and they were trembling. Very slowly, he lowered his head and drifted his mouth across hers, feeling it shiver and hearing the instinctive little escape of her breath. It was a lingering, unhurried whisper of a kiss, the brush of their lips the only point of contact. She had every opportunity to stop it but she did not.

Salvatore could feel his own desire building. He could sense her impatience, could hear the faint flutter of her hands as she tried to prevent herself from reaching out to touch him. Still he teased her with the merest whisper of a kiss until, with a small cry of her own surrender, Jessica reached up to clasp his face between both her hands.

'Oh, Salvatore,' she whispered brokenly. 'Salvatore.'

He stared deep into her eyes and nodded. 'Yes, *cara*. You have proved it to yourself. You want me, and I want you. It is so simple, isn't it? You are coming home with me,' he said softly, and thought that he disguised his triumph well.

Jessica stared up into the gleam of his brilliant eyes, her lips parting as he lowered his mouth to kiss her properly this time as the car sped off towards Chelsea.

CHAPTER SEVEN

THE front door closed behind them and Jessica stared at Salvatore, unsure of what to do next—out of her depth in a situation like this and weak and dizzy with the sensations which were sizzling over her skin.

She was vaguely aware that Salvatore's apartment was enormous and that there was the indefinable scent of luxury in the air, but luxury was the last thing on her mind as she gazed up at the man in front of her, wondering if this could really be happening to her. Her gorgeous boss staring down at her with the unmistakable look of sexual hunger on his face. What on earth did she do next?

Salvatore cupped her face in between both his hands, one thumb brushing against the pulse which fluttered furiously by the paper-thin skin at her temple. 'You are scared.'

It was an observation rather than a question and it sounded almost gentle. Jessica nodded. 'A little.'

'Am I to take it that you don't do this kind of thing very often?'

She shook her head. 'Never,' she whispered, slightly hurt that he should ask. And yet, who could blame him for asking—she hadn't exactly played hard to get, had she? Hadn't even stopped to think what she was getting into. 'Look, Salvatore, maybe this is crazy—'

But she got no further, for he had lowered his lips to brush against hers and his touch was intoxicating.

'No,' he murmured, breathing in her perfume. 'Not crazy at all. *Perfetto.* Perfect. It will be perfect—believe me, Jessica. Now let us get out of this inhospitable hall and go somewhere where we can be more at ease with one another.'

He laced her fingers with his and led her along a seemingly endless corridor, but inside Jessica's heart was racing. *At ease*, he had said, and yet she had never felt so nervous in her life. He was so confident, so sure of his own sexual power to assure her that this would be '*perfetto*'—but didn't he realise that he was dealing with someone who, while not a complete novice, wasn't exactly seasoned in the ways of making love?

Should she tell him so? And what could she say—that she was afraid she would disappoint him and was completely out of his league? Like a small, scruffy pony used to transporting schoolchildren round a field who had suddenly dared compete with a long-legged and aristocratic racehorse in the biggest race of the season?

But her throat was frozen as he led her into the biggest bedroom she'd ever seen, and no words of protest came.

She was aware of highly polished floors strewn with

beautiful faded rugs in different, muted colours. A silk-covered bed dominated a room which was big enough to accommodate a sofa and a couple of chairs, as well. An arched area led to a large study and she could see big pots crammed with amazing scarlet flowers and dark glossy foliage.

'Ah, Jessica,' Salvatore murmured as he drew her into his arms and stroked a tumble of shiny hair from her face. 'You look as though you are about to be thrown to the lions.'

'D-do I?'

'Mmm. Shall I be your lion? Your big, fierce lion?' his lips whispered to her neck. 'And shall I eat you up, every little bit of you, *cara mia*—would you like that?'

'Salvatore!' she exclaimed, but now she was trembling.

He smiled as he heard the faint shock in her voice, but deep down Salvatore approved of her lack of sophistication. Her relative innocence and reluctance were a welcome change from the lovers he had known in the past.

Unless it was all an act. A wide-eyed sham to make him 'respect' her more.

Pulling her a little closer, Salvatore skated his hands over her breasts and heard her breath quicken. Even if it was a sham—what did it matter? In the end, this was nothing but a temporary pursuit. Something to be enjoyed by both of them—and as long as she was fully aware of the rules, then nobody would get hurt...

He glanced down at her. Tonight she was wearing a purple silk dress with tiny buttons all the way down the front, which he began to undo, one by one.

'So many buttons! Did you wear this to deliberately tantalise me?' he teased.

Jessica could barely think, let alone speak, as he began to pop each one open and bare her heated flesh to the cooling wash of air. She had worn it because it was the most suitable thing that Willow had been able to find in her wardrobe.

His finger brushed along the edge of her bra—a plain and functional bra, he noted with an element of disapproval. But maybe there would be a lick of lace beneath.

'Salvatore,' she whispered, because by now the dress was open to her stomach, and he had bent down and was kissing her there—flicking his tongue into the gentle dip of her navel so that she gasped aloud and clutched at his broad shoulders.

And Salvatore gave a low laugh of delight. 'What is it, *cara mia*?' he questioned, his breath warm against her skin.

She wanted to tell him that she was terrified she would disappoint him, but no words came. 'I…I…'

'Just relax,' he murmured. 'Enjoy it.'

Somehow she did as he said, forgetting everything except the pleasure he was giving her as his tongue tracked slowly and erotically down over her belly. Desire began to grip at her in a way she had not experienced before. She felt it gathering pace, like a snowball getting bigger as you rolled it in fresh snow. She wanted him to…to…

But he didn't. The last button freed, he straightened up to slide the shirt-dress away from her narrow shoulders, so that she was left aching and hungry for him.

Salvatore saw the disappointment on her face and sensed her growing frustration, but he took his time. It was always best for the woman the first time if you made her wait. His eyes flicked over her. Despite her surprisingly expensive dress, her underwear was as disappointing as it had promised to be, plain and functional, her panties obscured by a hideous pair of tights. She would not wear those again, he thought grimly. 'Take off my shirt,' he ordered softly.

And Jessica, who was normally so good with her hands, now found that they would not obey this simple command at all. Had she thought he might take pity on her and remove the garment himself? But he did not. In fact, her struggle with freeing the buttons seemed to please him, until at last she slipped the shirt from his silken olive skin.

She swallowed. His golden-olive torso was formidable with not an ounce of spare flesh to be seen. He was all lean and honed muscle. So gorgeous. Too gorgeous, really. And if he asked her to take his trousers off, she would *die*.

But he didn't. He caught her against him, firmly and decisively—tangling his fingers in the thick gloss of her hair. And then he began to kiss her again, until she was soft and melting. He kissed her until her knees started to buckle and her hips began to make their own restless little circling against the formidable hardness of him. And still he kissed her, ignoring the growing clamour of her muffled little pleas for more. Until all her inhibitions had dissolved and she had begun to pluck impatiently at the belt of his trousers.

And only then did he smile, slip his fingers down the front of her panties and touch her with such unerring precision that she gave a loud gasp.

'Ah, *sì*,' he said softly, moving against her sweet heat. 'Now you are ready for love.'

Her blurred and hungry senses agreed, but his words sent questions dashing round her head. Love? Did this really have anything to do with love? wondered Jessica dazedly as he picked her up and carried her over to the bed. No, of course it didn't. Love was a word used to sweeten the act of sex.

She lay and watched him, as clearly he intended her to do. A slow and erotic striptease performed just for her benefit. His hand moved to his belt, and then his zip. He was pulling off his shoes, his socks, his trousers. He was stepping out of dark boxers with lazy elegance and he was aroused. Very aroused.

Their eyes met in one long moment and in that moment Jessica decided that nerves were no longer going to freeze her, because what would be the point of that? She was here and she was damned well going to enjoy every second of it. Every second of him.

'C-come to bed,' she said shakily.

He laughed softly as he joined her on the bed and she reached for him.

'You are hungry for me, little one?'

'I'm absolutely starving, if you must know!'

'Well, then—come here.' With one slick movement he removed her bra, then turned his attention to her naked breasts, first with his eyes and then letting his lips roam over their hard pink tips. He licked her, felt her shiver. 'Mmm. You taste of honey, and desire. You taste good.'

And his words made her *feel* good—so good that she wanted to throw inhibition to the wind. Shyly, she reached down to stroke him, feeling him jerk beneath her hand.

For one second, Salvatore stilled as something in her tentative gesture made a warning bell sound deep in his subconscious. He laid one hand over the fingers which lay so intimately over his flesh, mentally gearing himself up for a scenario which had only just occurred to him. And wondering how he could have been so stupid. For had not one of his beloved cousins been trapped by a woman in such a way?

'Please tell me you are not a virgin?' he demanded, his voice suddenly harsh.

Jessica didn't know whether to laugh or cry. Did that mean he equated her fumbling with a complete lack of experience? 'No, of course I'm not. Would it matter if I was?'

He took his hand away and moved over her, stroking her hair away from her face. 'Of course it would matter! But it is not important. Not now. Only this matters. *This*…'

And he blocked all words and thoughts with his lips. For a moment Jessica struggled against the wall of pleasure which was beginning to build, her thoughts uneasy as something in his attitude troubled her, though she wasn't quite sure what.

Quickly concern gave way to pleasure—how could it not, when Salvatore was the most wonderful lover imaginable? He kissed every inch of her body, she had never known that a man could find so much delight in the discovery of flesh alone.

'You like that?' he questioned silkily as his tongue found a particularly vulnerable area.

'I...' Jessica shut her eyes and shuddered. 'I...'

'Tell me,' he urged.

'No one has ever done that to me before,' she breathed.

'And this?'

'Oh, Salvatore,' she whispered. 'Yes.'

He took her along familiar pathways of delight and to his astonishment discovered that, for him, she was the perfect lover. So it was not a sham after all. She was not a virgin, but neither was she particularly accomplished. Inexperienced but not innocent—*perfetto*.

But she was also very sweet. Too sweet really, he thought wryly, as she pulled his head towards her and showered him with tiny kisses which made him tingle with delight. Did she not know that a woman should always hold something back in order to completely entrance a man?

'Jessica,' he said, in a voice which was suddenly unsteady, and he could wait no longer, he reached for protection as she writhed beneath him.

'Yes, now,' she whispered. 'Now.'

'Then damned well keep still for a minute!'

'I c-can't.'

'Neither can I,' he groaned as he thrust into her. *'Mia tesoro.'*

It was amazing. She was amazing—and he couldn't work out why. Was it her eagerness to please him? Her breathless pleasure as she worked out what made him moan with delight? Or her sheer joy when the first orgasm rocked her small, curvy body and she clung to him, choking out her pleasure and a few broken syllables which sounded a bit like his name?

Afterwards, Salvatore collapsed back against the disarray of pillows, his skin sweat-sheened, his heart racing like a piston as he stared at the ceiling, gasping for breath, like a man who had been pulled out of the water just before he drowned.

And Jessica snuggled up to him, resting her silky head in the crook of his arm as if that was the place she most wanted to be.

'Mmm,' she sighed. 'That was…*bliss*.'

A habitual post-lovemaking wariness began to creep over him. He was going to have to be very honest with her about the limitations of an affair with him—but surely she was sensible enough to recognise that there could be no future in this?

'Mmm.' He yawned, and edged away from her very fractionally. 'I'm hungry now, aren't you?'

She wanted to say, Not for food, I'm not—the way she would have done a few minutes ago, when they were making love and she seemed to have been given the most delicious freedom to indulge and tell him about every single one of her secret fantasies.

But something had changed—she could tell. Salvatore had withdrawn from her in more ways than one. It was true that in this bizarre situation she was probably being acutely sensitive, but it was quite clear that his mood towards her had changed, become cooler. What happened now—was she expected to get dressed and just go home?

'Shall I go and get us something to eat?' he questioned lazily.

And Jessica hated herself for the overwhelming sense of relief she felt that she wasn't to be dismissed like a servant. Hated herself even more for just accepting it—for allowing Salvatore to dictate the terms of what happened next.

But how could she do otherwise when she felt so blissfully *alive* in his arms—as if up until that moment her life had seemed without direction and the whole reason for being born had just been made clear to her?

'Yes, please,' she said, forcing herself down from the clouds. She'd barely touched a thing all weekend. She'd been to visit her grandmother, who had asked her if she was sickening for something when Jessica had done the unheard of and refused a slice of her famous lemon drizzle cake. But what could she have said to the much-loved woman who had brought her up after the death of her parents? No, I've lost my appetite because I think I'm going to end up in bed with my boss on Tuesday. Wouldn't that go against everything she'd been taught?

He flicked her an amused glance as he climbed out of bed, gloriously and goldenly assured in his nakedness. 'Thank heavens for that,' he murmured. 'A little loss of appetite in the restaurant was understandable—but I can't bear women who do sustained starvation as a matter of course.'

'Er, no. Neither can I.' Maybe she should pass that nugget of information on to Willow—who, of course, would never believe her. 'Should I get up?'

His eyes lingered over her. She looked deliciously tousled with her cheeks flushed pink and her grey eyes huge. 'No. Stay right there. You look enchanting. We'll have a picnic in bed.'

Once he'd gone, Jessica hurried into the bathroom and tried to tame her hair. Then she got back into bed and rather self-consciously sat there waiting for him until he returned carrying a tray loaded with expensive-looking goodies.

Champagne. Grapes. Some crusty-looking bread. And there was a lovely wooden box containing cheese—as well as a box of dark chocolate.

'That all looks wonderful,' she said brightly.

He heard the nerves in her voice and put the tray down and took her into his arms.

'You've brushed your hair,' he observed softly.

'Combed it. I borrowed your comb—I hope that was okay?'

Behind the tentative query, he heard a million other questions. From past displays of post-coital neediness, Salvatore knew that this was the most vulnerable time of all for a woman and the best time for ground rules to be laid down.

'You can borrow anything you like, while you're here,' he said easily.

The words should have reassured her, but they did just the opposite. Silently, Jessica acknowledged that she needed to know where she stood. At work, she might just be his office cleaner—but she had just shared his bed. Surely that gave her the right to know what he wanted from her?

'You asked me a question earlier,' she said.

Salvatore raised his brows. 'Which particular question was that?'

'You asked whether I was a virgin. Why?'

He had been about to trickle a finger from her stomach to the tempting fuzz of hair which lay at the fork of her thighs, but he resisted. If it was the truth she wanted, then he would give it to her. That way he couldn't be accused of having capitalised on sex to make her agree to something she would later throw back in his face.

'Because it would make a difference to what happened next,' he said, and went over to open the bottle—wishing now that he had brought something other than champagne, for that too could be misinterpreted. He said nothing until the liquid had foamed up inside the glasses in a creamy cascade, letting it settle before he topped them up. Then he walked back over to the bed and handed her a glass—though he put his own down on the bedside table, untouched.

'Thanks.' Jessica took the drink with a reluctance she hoped didn't show. It looked like ginger ale, and frankly, she wished it were ginger ale, for suddenly she felt peculiar, sitting naked in this billionaire's bed, drinking his champagne.

He sat down on the edge of the bed and looked at her.

'A woman's virginity is the greatest gift she can give to a man—apart from the children she will one day bear him.'

There were two outrageously old-fashioned concepts here, but for now only one concerned her. 'So…so what would the problem have been if I had been a virgin?'

He had hoped that she might have been able to work it out for herself without him having to spell it out. But he must—to do otherwise would be deception, and that he could not and would not tolerate.

'It would have been wasted on me,' he said softly. 'If you had been a virgin, I would have sent you away and told you to save that gift for the man you will one day marry.'

'But—'

'You see…' his blue eyes narrowed as he cut across her words, for there must be no misunderstanding on her part '…you must understand that I am Sicilian, Jessica, and that I have very strict values about life, as well as marriage. I intend to one day go back to Sicily, to marry a Sicilian girl who will be a virgin. That is a given.'

Jessica stared at him. Didn't he realise how that made her *feel* in the circumstances? More than a little bit cheap for having given herself to him so freely. And expendable, too. No, of course he didn't—why should he?

'That's so old-fashioned.'

He shrugged. 'I recognise that, but I don't care. In many ways, I am a very old-fashioned man. For me it is important that the mother of my children has not…how do you say? Been around the block?'

Jessica sat bolt upright, some champagne spilling on the rumpled cotton sheets, but she didn't care as she swung her legs over the bed and put the glass down with a trembling hand. 'How dare you?' she demanded shakily. 'How dare you accuse me of sleeping around, when actually I *haven't*—and you've probably had more women than I've had hot dinners and, oh…*oh*!'

Her furious words were silenced with a kiss, because Salvatore had moved even faster and caught her in his arms as he tumbled her back on the bed, his silk robe falling open and his unashamedly aroused body moulding itself against hers.

'Get off me!' she exclaimed, drumming her fists furiously against his chest. 'Get *off* me!'

'You want me to?'

'Yes! No. *Yes*!' But her words belied her actions because her eyelids were fluttering closed and she could feel the instant clamour of desire.

'Jessica?'

She opened her eyes and stared at him with the caution of a hunted animal which knew it was cornered. 'What?'

'I make you no false promises,' he said simply. 'Nor spin you any false lies. I like you. That's why you are here. I like making love to you. I'd like to do it again. I'd like to spoil you a little. To fly you to Paris and feed you with oysters. To show you a little of the world you do not yet know—and I think you'd like that, too.'

As his words painted a tempting picture Jessica stared at him in confusion, aware of the frantic hammering of her heart and the way that her breasts were peaking insistently against his chest—as if eager to be touched by him. As if her body were impatient with her questions, but she knew she had to ask him.

'I don't understand,' she breathed. 'What is it you want from me?'

Salvatore gave a swift, hard smile, recognising that her inexperience was a double-edged sword. It attracted him—but it made explanation necessary, and he liked to keep explanation to a minimum.

He fixed her in his gaze, staring down at her wide grey eyes and the parted rose-petal lips. 'I want you to be my mistress,' he said softly.

CHAPTER EIGHT

STILL tangled against his naked body, Jessica stared up into the blue of Salvatore's eyes and for a moment thought she might have misheard him. 'Your mistress?' she echoed, because in her world men didn't come out and say things like that. 'But you're not even *married*!' Her eyes narrowed suspiciously as a terrible thought occurred to her and she wondered why it had never entered her mind before. 'Are you?'

He shook his head, a wry smile curving his lips. 'No, I am not married, *cara*—but a man does not need to be married to require a mistress.' He saw the confusion on her face, and he stoked it. 'It is nothing but a title given to a woman who fulfils a special role in a man's life. Mainly, it does away with uncertainty and means that we both know exactly where we stand. And where we stand is to have a wonderful affair while accepting that there is no future in it. That's all.'

She blinked. 'That's all?' she repeated.

'That is over-simplifying it a little, perhaps,' he admitted. 'But essentially that is what it is—and what is more I think that you are utterly perfect for the role, *cara*.'

The word 'perfect' was a verbal caress, accompanied by the whisper of his lips as they trailed along the line of her jaw, causing Jessica to shiver with longing. She was so weak in his arms; she imagined that every woman would be. Yet how could she even consider what he had just proposed? Wasn't such a bald proposition hugely insulting?

He raised his head to stroke the outline of her lips with a questing fingertip. 'You do not answer,' he observed.

She heard the unmistakable surprise in his voice and somehow that irritated her. Did he really expect her to fall upon a suggestion that many women would dismiss out of hand—perhaps even be *grateful* to him for asking?

'It's...it's a lot to take in,' she said, wondering why he'd said anything at all. Why couldn't he have just made love to her and taken her out again? Why couldn't it have just drifted on in the normal way between a man and a woman, if he had really enjoyed it as much as he claimed?

Because then you might start getting the wrong idea, you idiot! You might start thinking that you had some kind of future with him, and he is making it crystal clear from the very start that nothing like that is going to happen.

Without warning, he lowered his head, his mouth replacing his fingertip with a lingering kiss, and Jessica tried for a moment to resist him. But it was just a moment—her body was greedy for him, warm and soft as she welcomed him in.

'Che voglia,' he said, his voice suddenly harsh.

She gasped as he entered her, their eyes meeting in a long unspoken moment.

Salvatore looked down at her and felt desire overpower him. 'It's good?' he questioned unsteadily.

'Y-yes,' she trembled.

'You want more?'

'You know I do,' she whispered, as vulnerable then as she had ever been.

Deeply, he thrust inside her, hearing her gasp again, watching her face as passion melted away the last of her lingering doubts and listening as her eventual shuddering little cries pierced the air. Only then did he allow himself to let go, falling over into a place of incredible sweetness—made sweeter still by a victory he should not have had to press for with a woman like Jessica.

Afterwards, they lay spent in each other's arms. Salvatore stroked lazily at her soft skin, still damp with exertion as he inhaled her flowery perfume, which was now mixed with his own raw, elemental scent. His touch was abstracted and his thoughts had drifted far away, for she had surprised him.

She had viewed his proposition with a remarkably cool restraint—weighing it up with all the consideration which he himself might have given to a business proposal. Why, he knew society beauties and heiresses who would have bitten his hand off to grace his bed like this! And she still hadn't given him an answer, he realised.

'You are sleepy?' he questioned.

Jessica opened her eyes. Yes, her body was tired, but her mind was racing, and feigning sleep was easier than having to face up to the uncomfortable reality of the situation. What should she do? 'A little.'

'We still haven't had any supper,' he observed.

'No.' Jessica sat up, seeing his eyes transfixed by her naked breasts, and in a way that helped her make up her mind. He saw her as a body—something that he desired. She fed his sexual appetite just as the bread and cheese would soon feed a more elemental hunger. As long as she didn't forget that, then surely she could protect her heart against being broken? 'So perhaps we'd better have something to eat,' she said softly. 'And then I'll get going.'

Salvatore stilled. 'Going?' he echoed the word in soft disbelief. 'Going where?'

Jessica looked at him. 'Why, home, of course.'

Now he was taken aback, a state of being completely unknown to him. Usually, he could read a woman like a well-thumbed book, but for once in his life he was perplexed. Was the inconceivable happening? Was Jessica Martin *walking out*? He felt the flicker of a pulse at his temple. If she was trying to test him, then she would soon discover that he would not be manipulated!

'Why home?' he questioned silkily.

At least he had managed to tear his eyes away from her breasts and was actually looking at her face! 'Because it's a Tuesday night and I've got work tomorrow morning.'

Salvatore leaned back against the pillows. 'So what's the problem? Stay the night here and I'll have my driver drop you off at your office in the morning.'

Jessica looked at him and, despite the see-sawing of

her emotions, she couldn't help a smile from nudging at her lips. Oh, yes—that was an absolutely brilliant idea. She could just imagine the helpful kind of gossip *that* would produce! Her turning up for work in a chauffeur-driven limousine wearing last night's make-up!

'It's very sweet of you, Salvatore,' she said softly. 'But I don't think it's such a good idea.'

'Why not?' he snapped.

'Well, for a start, I haven't brought a change of clothes with me.'

'And why not? You didn't think you would end up in bed with me tonight? We both knew it was on the cards,' he accused hotly.

Jessica met the furious blaze in his eyes, but she didn't flinch—even though his words were far from flattering. 'Well, yes. I suppose I did.'

'Then why the hell didn't you bring something with you? A change of clothes? A toothbrush?'

Didn't he know *anything* about women? 'Because that would have looked so…so obvious, wouldn't it? If I'd turned up for a dinner-date clutching a small overnight bag! Listen…' she leaned over and kissed him briefly on the lips '…I'll have some supper with you first and then I'll go home. That way, you'll get a good night's sleep, and so will I.'

He glared at her. 'You sound like my nurse!'

Her mouth crumpled into a smile. 'If I were your nurse, Salvatore—then I would just have broken my professional code rather spectacularly,' she teased.

Salvatore frowned. In a way, he couldn't fault her logic

and yet he had never felt quite so wrong-footed in his life. *She* was outlining her plan of action to *him*—instead of hanging onto his every word and waiting to hear what his wishes were? It was unimaginable! His cleaner!

'You are playing the coquette with me?' he growled. 'Is that it?'

Jessica giggled, suddenly feeling more than a little bit high—unsure whether that was the result of the most fantastic lovemaking of her life or drinking champagne on an empty stomach. 'It's a little late in the day for playing hard to get, isn't it?' She reached down for the plate of grapes and popped one in her mouth, holding another up in front of his. 'Here. Have one.'

'I don't want a damned grape,' he growled. Suddenly, he needed a drink. Incredulously, he watched as she slid off the bed. It had not been an idle threat after all. 'So you really are going?'

Jessica turned round, trying not to feel self-conscious in her nakedness—but having no clothes on when you were in bed with a man was one thing, having to walk across the room to retrieve your discarded clothing was another. 'Yes.'

Briefly, he contemplated getting up and going after her, of perhaps pinning her up against the wall and making her gasp his name out loud. But he recognised that, although he could easily delay her, he wasn't going to stop her from leaving. Despite the fact that she must know she was displeasing him, he could see the unmistakable look of determination which had tightened those rose-petal lips of hers.

Jessica picked up her panties and slithered into them, and clipped her bra closed, wondering how on earth strippers managed to do this kind of thing erotically, and in a room full of strangers, too. She picked up the pair of tights. Though maybe it was easier in front of strangers. Just pretend he isn't watching you with that predatory stare, she told herself as she struggled into them.

'Jessica?'

She looked up as the elastic pinged round her waist. 'Yes, Salvatore.'

His mouth curved with undisguised distaste. 'You will not wear those *things* again when you are with me.'

'Tights?'

'Yes. *Tights.*' He shuddered. 'Whoever invented them should be shot. Women should wear nothing but lacy stockings, and suspender belts.'

'I'll bear it in mind,' said Jessica gravely as she picked up the purple silk dress and pulled it over her head, glad of the distraction of doing that for fear that he might read the slightly sad fact in her eyes. That she'd never actually worn stockings and a suspender belt before. Wouldn't that be a shocking admission?

'Make sure you do,' he said coolly as, with the naturally critical eye which most Sicilian men possessed, Salvatore assessed her. The purple silk dress suited her very well, he thought, since it clung enticingly to her curves. But the length was all wrong.

'And why do you wear your dresses so long?' he questioned idly.

Jessica blushed. 'You don't like it?'

His gaze travelled slowly from toe to thigh, and lingered there. 'It hides your legs—your beautiful legs. Why hide one of your best assets?'

She hesitated. Should she tell him? Did he actually want the truth—for her to paint an accurate picture of her life so that he could see her as she really was, warts and all?

'It's Willow's dress,' she said.

'Willow?' He frowned. 'This is the tree, *sì*? It lives along the riverbank?'

'My housemate,' Jessica elaborated and was slightly horrified at the feeling of relief which shot through her. He hadn't even remembered the name of her stunning blonde housemate! 'She's taller than me.'

Still he looked blank.

'It's her dress I'm wearing. Willow's dress. I borrowed it.'

And suddenly Salvatore felt better. Much better—because this was stuff he could deal with, stuff he could understand. He watched as Jessica did up the final button and then ran her fingers through her hair. Maybe she was cleverer than he had given her credit for—or maybe it was just coincidence that she had told him now—but this nugget of information gave him back the familiar feel of power and control.

Had she worn the dress to get precisely this result? That he would take pity on her and shower gifts on her? It wouldn't be the first time it had happened, but at least it made the playing field more level.

He put his empty glass down and got up from the bed,

seeing her eyes darken with desire and apprehension as he began to walk across the large bedroom towards her. And when he had reached her, he lifted both her hands to his lips and kissed each fingertip in turn—like a man playing a harmonica.

'I don't want you wearing second-hand clothes any more,' he said silkily.

Jessica opened her mouth to tell him it wasn't as easy as that. That most of the items in *her* wardrobe were completely unsuitable for the kind of place Salvatore frequented, but he forestalled her with a swift shake of his ruffled dark head.

'I know what you're going to say.' He dropped his hands to allow his fingers to roam expertly over the fine, slippery material which covered her bottom. 'That you can't afford to buy clothes of this quality.'

'Well, I can't,' said Jessica proudly.

'And one of the many advantages of being mistress to a rich man,' he purred, 'is that I can.'

She shook her head. 'No!'

'Oh, yes. Do not protest, Jessica—for your protests are unnecessary. You see—' his voice deepened '—it will give me great pleasure to buy for you, and to dress you—from the skin up.' He touched the silk, tracing a light line over her breast, smiling as she shivered—despite the mutinous look on her face. 'I do not want you wearing these ugly little bra and panties any more, either.'

She felt as if he were tearing her up into little pieces before putting her back together again. 'If how I look is so disappointing to you, then why don't you go off and find someone whose looks *do* appeal?'

'You appeal to me very much,' he said softly. 'But you are like one of the trees in my orchard back home in Sicily. You need to be pruned before you can blossom properly. Now come here.'

'Salvatore—' But he was teasing her with his kiss, pulling her closer into his warm naked body—hard up against the unmistakable force of his renewed arousal. 'You still wish to go?'

She closed her eyes. How easy it would be to say no. To allow herself to be undressed once more and made love to. But it would be a sign of weakness, surely, showing him that she could be manipulated to his will whenever it suited him. And she would *not* go into work tomorrow resplendent in a gaudy party dress.

'I must.'

His mouth hardened. 'Very well. So be it. I will notify my driver.'

Jessica felt anxious as he picked up a phone and bit out a command—and when he had finished he turned to her, an odd kind of smile on his face, his blue eyes glittering with a message she couldn't read.

'I'll call you,' he said.

She wanted to say, When? But suddenly Jessica felt disorientated. Did any of the normal rules of dating apply when you agreed to become a rich man's mistress, or did he call all the shots? She bent down towards her handbag. Who was she kidding? Of course he called all the shots—in just about every area of his life.

'Goodnight, Salvatore,' she said, and, picking up her handbag, she hurried towards the door before he could see any of the gnawing anxieties which were eating her up.

CHAPTER NINE

'WHAT do you mean—his *mistress*?' Willow demanded.

Jessica stared down at the cereal which was growing soggy in the bowl of milk and stirred at it uninterestedly with her spoon. She shouldn't have said anything to her housemate. *Why* had she opened her big mouth and confided Salvatore's shockingly erotic proposition? Because you had to tell someone or you'd go crazy and burst!

'Oh, it's a kind of arrangement that men make with women all the time,' she said, shrugging her shoulders in an airy manner, as if she were used to dealing with such concepts every day of the week.

'You mean it allows him to behave exactly as he wants to behave without having any responsibilities towards the woman!' flared Willow. 'Why the hell did you agree to it, Jessica? I take it you *did* agree to it?'

'I guess I did,' she said slowly.

'But *why*? Are you out of your mind?'

'Because…because…' Jessica bit her lip. Because she adored him. Because a camaraderie had built up between them since she'd been working for him and that had contributed towards the way she had seized on this opportunity.

'Because what?' prompted Willow.

Jessica pushed the untouched cereal away and stared at her housemate, her blonde hair tumbling all over her shoulders, her porcelain skin flawless without a scrap of make-up. She wondered whether Willow was just being naïve, or mischievous. 'Are you trying to tell me that you *wouldn't* have succumbed to his charms?'

'I'd have made him wait.'

'Yeah, sure you would.' Jessica clamped her lips shut. She would never ever dream of telling another woman of what had gone on behind closed doors, but surely Willow must realise that there were some men who were simply impossible to resist, and Salvatore was one of them.

'But I wonder why he chose *you*,' pondered Willow thoughtfully, and it was only when she saw the expression on Jessica's face that she attempted to take some of the sting out of the question. 'I mean—isn't it a bit risky, Jessica? You work there, and everything.'

'You mean I clean his office,' said Jessica, her cheeks flushing with defiant pride. 'And if you really want to know why I think he chose me, Willow…' Because surely if you forced yourself to face the fundamental truth in a situation, then you removed its ability to cause you pain? It was only when you ran from the truth that you were in trouble.

'I think it's precisely because I *do* clean his office,' she continued slowly. 'I know my place and I'm not a threat. We can have...*fun*...but without him worrying that he might have to make some kind of commitment to me.' She forced herself to remember his stark words about going back to marry a Sicilian virgin. 'Because it isn't going to happen.'

'And did he...' Willow began to fiddle self-consciously with her hair '...did he happen to mention me?'

A crueller person than Jessica might have rubbed it in that the Sicilian hadn't even remembered Willow's name. But Jessica was not cruel, and anyway she doubted that the sunnily confident blonde would have believed her. 'No, he didn't,' she answered quietly. 'Should he have done?'

Willow carefully fielded the question with another of her own. 'So when are you seeing him again? Or maybe you don't know. Can he just ring out for you at a moment's notice—like pizza?'

Jessica didn't react. She was *not* going to rise to it. But didn't Willow's taunt only feed her own terrible fears? 'He's been away—on business. He travels such a lot. He's in New York this week.'

'How nice for him. So did you see him before he left?'

'Briefly,' said Jessica. She had been stricken with nerves, terrified about going in to clean his office, not knowing how she would face him or what she would say to him after what had happened between them.

But after all that angsting, he hadn't even been there—the room had been quiet and empty and she hadn't known whether to laugh or cry. Instead, she had busied herself by cleaning up the vast space, scrubbing at the surfaces even more energetically than usual and resisting the temptation to snoop around in his desk—something which had never occurred to her before she'd slept with him. She had just been coming out of the adjoining cloakroom with a damp cloth in her hand when the door had opened and in he'd walked.

He had been wearing a dark suit, which intensified the deep ebony of his black hair, and the blue of his eyes looked unbelievably bright—set like sapphires in his glowing olive skin. He had put his briefcase down, and looked at her for a long moment.

'Jessica,' he said.

She really didn't know how to react. She wanted to run into his arms, to stroke his glowing skin, to touch him wonderingly as if she couldn't quite believe he was real. But she didn't dare do anything except stand there in her stupid pink overall.

'Come over here,' he ordered softly.

The cloth must have somehow slipped from her fingers by the time she reached him, but he lifted up her hands and looked wryly at the bright yellow rubber gloves she wore.

'I've never been able to understand the sexual allure of rubber,' he said, almost conversationally, as he began to pull off the gloves which had stuck unflatteringly to her fingers. When he had peeled them off, he tossed them aside and took her into his arms, his blue eyes dancing. 'Have you?'

'N-no. I've...never really given it any thought.'

He lifted her chin and frowned. 'You are nervous,' he observed.

Jessica nodded. No point in denying it when it was as obvious as the huge moon which looked like a stage prop shining outside the penthouse window. 'A little bit,' she whispered.

'And yet we have been deliciously intimate with each other,' he mused. 'With the promise of so much more. Are you angry because I haven't rung you?'

'You haven't got my phone number,' Jessica replied, more pointedly than she had intended.

His blue eyes gleamed. 'You think that would be a problem, *cara*? That I could not find you if I wished to find you?'

She supposed not. But it gave Jessica an insight into the kind of man she was dealing with. The kind of man who could get just about any information with a click of his powerful fingers.

'Now kiss me,' he murmured.

Had she been afraid—and half hoping—that he would sandwich in a bout of fast and furious sex with her, before he left for the airfield where his plane was waiting?

But to Jessica's surprise, he did not. Maybe he didn't have time for a shower in the luxury cloakroom which adjoined the penthouse office, or maybe he didn't want to crease his immaculate suit. Or maybe, unlike her, he didn't allow a lover to dominate his thoughts. Whereas she had been able to think of nothing but him, it seemed that she had barely even crossed his mind.

Yet the kiss was sweet. Unbearably sweet. Kisses could be more poignant than anything else, she found herself thinking, her heart aching. His kiss made her wish that he weren't Salvatore Cardini, boss of one of the biggest corporations in the world. It made her wish he were just an ordinary man—not a glittering star who was way out of her reach. If he were an accountant, say, that she'd met at one of the city's bars, wouldn't that have been just so much easier? They would go back to her flat, or his—and she would cook spaghetti bolognese and they'd drink a bottle of cheap plonk.

There would be no unrealistic expectations, no worries about what to wear or whether she would say the wrong thing if he took her out somewhere. And no fears already creeping in as she wondered just how long this would all last.

'When are you back?' she asked him in spite of having vowed not to do any such thing.

'I'll be back by the weekend.' His mouth curved in a smile as he looked down into her eyes 'Are we going to see one another?'

'I hope so,' she said shyly.

Her words made him halt, stroke her hair almost reflectively. 'Okay, Jessica—I'll be in touch.'

And with another brief and tantalising kiss, he disappeared, leaving her looking after him with a feeling of longing and realisation that she would never be anything but a peripheral person in his life.

'So when are you seeing him?' Willow's words prompted Jessica back to the present with a jolt and with a blink she looked up at the bright yellow clock which was hanging on the kitchen wall.

'He's collecting me any minute now.'

'Then oughtn't you be getting ready?'

'I *am* ready.'

Willow's face froze. 'Oh.'

But Salvatore had criticised her borrowed clothes and Jessica had decided that she wasn't going to borrow any more of them. Consequently, she was wearing her favourite pair of jeans. They were old and rather faded, but a perfect fit, and with them she'd put on a soft grey cashmere sweater bought in last year's January sale. A black velvet ribbon caught her hair back in a loose ponytail and she wore the minimum amount of make-up.

Outwardly, she was trying to project a calm exterior, but inside she was quaking with nerves and exhilaration at the thought of seeing him again.

There was a loud knock on the door and Jessica opened it to Salvatore's driver. Behind him the limousine dominated the small road and through the smoked glass she could see Salvatore talking into his cell phone.

'Signor Cardini is just finishing a call from Milan,' explained the driver.

Jessica picked up her jacket, her expression just *defying* Willow to make some smart comment, but she said nothing.

'That's fine,' she said brightly, and walked out to the waiting limousine.

Salvatore was sprawled in the back seat and when he saw her he said something very quickly in Italian, and terminated the conversation.

'*Ciao, bella,*' he murmured silkily. 'Come over here and say hello to me.'

His eyes were glittering over her in an unashamedly sexual appraisal, making her feel a little like a trophy. But suddenly Jessica didn't care. Wasn't this what she had been dreaming about since the last time she'd been out with him? She scrambled into his arms like a puppy reunited with its master as the driver closed the door behind her.

'Mmm.' Salvatore felt the kick of lust as he lowered his mouth to kiss her. She tasted of toothpaste, as if she was fresh from the bath. She tasted clean and pure—with that strange innocence which was all her own. He gave a little groan as he drove his mouth down on hers, his hand skimming down over one denim-clad hip—and when eventually he broke the kiss, it was to raise his head to look down at her with smoky blue eyes.

'I'm taking you straight home because I've spent the last five days imagining making love to you,' he promised unsteadily.

'I can't wait,' she breathed, locking her arms tightly around his neck.

'I can tell,' he mocked, but she simply lifted her lips to kiss him again and he gave a low laugh of pleasure. He had chosen his mistress well. In his arms she was utterly inhibited—like a wild little foal eager to be trained. He wanted to touch her now, maybe to bring her to climax within the private world of the dark-windowed limousine, but she was wearing jeans.

He let his fingers splay into a possessive star at the very top of her thigh, hearing her breathing quicken, but his eyes mocked her. 'These jeans are so inhibiting,' he observed caustically.

'But so practical.'

'On the contrary,' he said. 'They are extremely *impractical* for lovers who are being reunited.'

Suddenly Jessica felt about eighteen years old.

'You have never had instruction on how best to dress to please a man?' he persisted softly.

'It's not usually part of an English education.'

'Then I shall teach you,' he promised. 'And I shall take you shopping.'

'To kit me out as befits the mistress of a wealthy man?'

'Precisely that, *cara mia*.'

'And what if I tell you that I won't let you buy me anything?' she questioned proudly.

'Then I will ride roughshod over your wishes,' he murmured throatily, his finger fixed on the tip of her chin so that she couldn't escape the erotic question in his eyes. 'Do you think you'd enjoy me riding roughshod, *cara*?'

Predictably, she blushed, and just as predictably that made him kiss her again.

'Oh, oh, Salvatore...*you*...*you*...!'

'Oh, you what, *cara*?' he breathed back as he put his hands underneath her sweater and began to caress her.

She wanted to tell him that she was here, in his arms, because she wanted to be—not because of what she could get out of him. But by then the car had reached the pretty Chelsea street where he lived.

By daylight it looked quite different. It was exquisite, lined with trees which would soon bear blossom in the springtime. Would he have flown away by then and gone off to warmer climes? she wondered. Back to Sicily to choose his pure bride, leaving Jessica with nothing but sweet memories and an empty future?

The apartment looked bigger by daylight, too—and far more luxurious than Jessica remembered. Every piece of furniture looked as carefully chosen as a work of art, every surface gleamed with attention. Who cleaned his apartment for him? she found herself wondering.

'Did you choose these pieces yourself?' she questioned, running her finger along the curving line of a small sofa which looked far too beautiful to sit on.

His eyes narrowed. Had she started taking an inventory of how much he was worth? 'I had someone buy them for me,' he said casually. 'Someone who is an expert in antiques and interiors. I spoke to her on the phone, told her what I liked and disliked—she flew to Milan to take a look at the apartment I owned there and from that she came up with this.'

'And you like it?'

'I love it.' His voice was smooth. 'Don't you?'

'Oh, yes,' said Jessica, feeling a little unsteady. It was such a weird way to live your life, she thought—and so different from hers. You could buy anything, she realised. Expertise. Tables in exclusive restaurants.

Quickly, she walked past a beautiful painting she would normally have spent ages looking at, and went instead to the window and the pale expanse of the winter sky. The view of the river was beautiful and calming—though even that too carried a very expensive price tag.

Salvatore came up behind her, his hands on her shoulders as he pressed his body against her back and whispered his lips to her neck.

'What's up? Your shoulders look all tense and you were miles away,' he murmured.

A whole world away, she thought, but what would be the point in spoiling it? That would be like someone failing to appreciate the beauty of a rainbow, on the grounds that it didn't last long enough!

She turned round in his arms and lifted her face up to his. 'I'm here now,' she whispered.

But through the heavy beat of building desire, Salvatore felt a faint sense of misgiving, even as he slid his hands underneath her grey sweater and cupped her soft breasts. Did those shining eyes of hers reproach him, or was that his own, guilty conscience?

But you've got nothing to be guilty for!

They were both consenting adults who had gone into this with their eyes open—and if Jessica was a different breed from the city-sophisticates he ran across in his daily life, then why not just lie back and enjoy the difference?

But as he guided her hand towards his belt he felt a sudden fleeting wish that she was one of those women, with their experienced eyes and experienced hands. Someone who wouldn't look at him with that crazy mixture of tenderness and enthusiasm. Didn't she realise that such feelings were a total waste of her time and that he would not be swayed by them?

His mouth hardened. He must teach her how he liked his women to behave.

CHAPTER TEN

'WE OUGHT to think about getting up.'

Lazily, Salvatore opened his eyes and yawned. 'Why?'

'Because…' Jessica tried to put her thoughts into some kind of coherent order, but it wasn't easy when there was a naked man in bed beside you who possessed her Sicilian lover's impressive physique. One golden and muscular thigh lay sprawled over one of hers, pinning her to the bed, making her achingly aware of the strong, warm weight of his body. 'Because we've been in bed nearly all day,' she blurted out. 'That's all we ever seem to do.'

He smiled, whispering a finger with idle precision over one breast and seeing her automatic shiver of delight and desire. 'And what is wrong with that, *mia cara*? In bed we can talk, we can sleep, eat—and of course make love. Can you think of a place you would prefer to be?'

Jessica stared into the bright blue eyes, feeling her stomach turn to water as he stroked her so expertly. 'Well, no. I suppose when you put it like that, I can't.'

'So what's the problem?'

The problem was that Jessica felt as if she was building up an addiction to her Sicilian lover and she couldn't see how she was ever going to conquer it. Like someone who had never tasted chocolate and had then been given a huge boxful and told to eat as many as she liked—she couldn't seem to stop herself. The lazy days they spent in each other's arms only intensified her perception of the two of them as a unit; the two of them in their own little world. And two months as Salvatore's mistress had only increased her desire for him to a dangerously high pitch.

'I can't really think properly when you're touching me like that,' she complained weakly.

'Then don't think. Just feel. Just like that. And that feels good, doesn't it, Jessica?'

'You…you know it does.'

He made love to her slowly, luxuriously—revelling in the way she reacted to him. She did not shy away from showing her delight, or her thanks. Each time he gave her pleasure she behaved as if she had just been given a precious gift. She was the sweetest lover he had ever known, he reflected.

He kissed the tip of her nose and stared down into her face. Her cheeks were flushed and her thick, shiny hair lay spread all over his pillow—her parted lips always looking as if they wanted to be kissed. Her eagerness had captivated him in a way he had not expected to be captivated—and yet he was naturally wary. 'You have not slept with many men, I think?' he questioned thoughtfully.

Jessica stilled. Was that supposed to be a criticism—that she had in some way disappointed him? And what had made him come out with it now?

'You mean I'm no good?'

He shook his head. 'Most emphatically I did not mean that, *cara*.'

'Then how? How can you tell?'

He shrugged as he circled his hand over the flat of her belly, ignoring her wriggling little unspoken request that his hand travel down further still. 'It is difficult to put into words,' he said slowly. 'You are quick to learn and eager to please and yet you are not as so many women are—so experienced that they treat the act of love as if they were eating a meal, that they always do *this* first, and then they always do *that*. You understand?'

Jessica nodded. 'I think so.' She bit her lip, suddenly shy. 'It makes me aware of how many different women you must have had.'

His smile was indulgent as his fingertips continued their tantalisingly slow journey. 'Probably not as many as you would imagine—but, *sì*, of course there have been women. What else would you expect, *mia tesoro*—when I am a man of thirty-six years?'

'I suppose.'

'How *many* lovers?' he demanded suddenly, his fingers halting.

For a moment Jessica looked at him blankly, not knowing what he meant.

'How many lovers have you had?' he questioned.

She wanted to say that he had no right to ask her a

question like that, but deep down she knew she wanted to redeem herself in his harshly judgemental eyes—to let him know that there had not been a long line of men in her past. 'Only one,' she admitted.

His eyes narrowed as he took in the implications of her words. 'You were in love with him?'

She shrugged. What she had felt for William had been a pale imitation of what she felt for Salvatore. 'I thought I was at the time.'

'Ah.' He nodded. 'It is a pity,' he said slowly, 'that you did not wait—that you wasted your innocence on a man who is now in your past.'

Jessica blinked. *'Wasted?'*

'*Sì*. Of course. Then you would have had the perfect gift to offer to your husband on your wedding night.' His lips curved into a soft smile. 'But then, of course, you would not be in bed with me, *cara mia*.'

Jessica counted to ten, trying to remind herself that at heart he was a Sicilian—hard and unyielding and uncompromising. She wouldn't ever change him—so what was the point of having this kind of insulting conversation again and again?

She had to keep her face from crumpling as his cruel words brought home just how temporary this arrangement was. And if you keep allowing your emotions to get involved, then you are going to end up very badly hurt, Jessica.

The trouble was that she suspected it was already too late. She was already in much too deep. And where was it going to lead her? Precisely nowhere. She might be spinning all kinds of foolish fantasies about him, but he sure as hell wasn't doing the same thing about her! In fact, he would be horrified if he could read her mind and her dreamy thoughts about him.

So start behaving like a mistress should, instead of some weak little victim who's desperate for a crumb of love he will never throw in your direction.

Putting her arms above her head, Jessica stretched and yawned, knowing that the movement extended her body like a taut bow and seeing from the darkening of his eyes that the gesture had not escaped him. Surely playing out the kind of fantasy a man like him would expect couldn't be *that* difficult?

'Didn't you say something about shopping?' she questioned in a lilting voice.

Salvatore's eyes narrowed. Yes, he had—but her comment took him completely by surprise. In the past, she had brushed off his suggestions that she allow him to buy her some clothes—and since they had spent most of their time in bed, there hadn't been the necessity to do so.

Had that simply been a clever ruse on Jessica's part, he wondered—to lull him into thinking that she was uninterested in his money? Had she played the oldest trick known to man—of first ensnaring him with her body before moving in for the financial kill? And had he, Salvatore Cardini, been stupid enough to fall for it?

'*Sì, cara*—I should love to choose your wardrobe for you,' he said silkily.

Jessica thought she heard a flicker of warning in his voice. But wasn't this what he wanted—to dress her up like a doll, so that she would be fit to enter the finest salons in London? Hadn't he been on about it for days now? 'Didn't you say that there was a big dinner next week that you wanted me to attend?'

Salvatore propped himself up on his elbows. 'Indeed I did,' he agreed slowly, his eyes travelling over her pink and white curves. 'So why don't you put your clothes on, and we'll go out and buy you something to wear?'

But, disconcertingly, his voice had a new, hard edge to it. Jessica slid her legs over the side of the bed, aware that his blue eyes were watching her with unsmiling scrutiny—as if she had just agreed to some unspoken transaction and now she was expected to play her part in it.

Nervously, her tongue flicked out to moisten her lips as she pulled on her functional panties and the plain bra, trying to make it look as erotic as possible, but her nerve was evaporating like water spilt on a hot pavement.

How could she possibly compete with all those women he'd known in the past? Women of his own class—rich women—who could afford to clothe their bodies in the finest silks and satins, the kind of underwear of which he had spoken so longingly the first time they'd been to bed together.

Salvatore felt his body stir yet again as he watched her and it was as if someone had just removed the blinkers from his eyes. Oh, but she was good. The way she snaked her tongue out to make her lips gleam at him so provocatively. That innocent little flutter of her eyelashes. The coy way she half turned her back to make him achingly aware of the high swell of her bottom.

'Come over here,' he said.

'But...but you said—'

'I said, come over here.'

Despite the sudden harshness in his voice, she couldn't resist him even though she could see exactly what he wanted from the smoky look of desire in his blue eyes as he looked at her. You're just an object in his eyes, she told herself—but knowing that didn't stop her.

He reached up and pulled her down on top of him and instantly she could feel his arousal pressing against her as his fingers began tugging impatiently at her underwear.

'Salvatore,' she whispered. 'I've only just put them on.'

'Then let's get rid of them once and for all. Didn't you say you wanted new ones?' His voice was as rough as his gesture as he hooked the panties between his hands and ripped them apart.

'S-Salvatore—' It should have felt just like erotic play, but it did not. Suddenly it felt very different indeed, and as Jessica gazed up into his eyes they became hooded, guarded. But he caught her by the hips, brought her up close, and then he was thrusting into her and it was too late to do anything other than to bite out her pleasure.

It was fast and it was highly charged and Jessica found herself sobbing out her fulfilment just before Salvatore followed her with a strange, almost bitter cry.

Afterwards she lay beside him, gulping air back into her starved lungs as she became aware not just of the rapid thundering of her heart, but that he was not cradling her against his chest, nor stroking her hair as he usually did.

How strange sex could be, Jessica thought. Sometimes it could make you feel so close to someone, and sometimes it could make you feel completely distant.

Like now.

She turned her head to the side as she felt him move. Salvatore was getting up, uncurling his body like a large and very elegant cat—but he didn't say a word, just headed for the shower, and she lay there wondering what it was that had made him so suddenly moody.

Well, don't, she told herself firmly as she got out of bed and went to use one of the other bathrooms. Sensitivity isn't going to get you anywhere.

She showered and dressed and when she reappeared Salvatore was waiting for her. And although he still had that rather forbidding look on his face, she went straight over to him and looped her arms around his neck. Because, otherwise, what was the point in all this?

'I had the most gorgeous shower,' she whispered.

He could tell. She smelt of violets and jasmine and her shiny hair was still faintly damp. He tried to tell himself that now that she had a shopping trip in her line of fire, there was going to be no stopping her—but he hadn't counted on that soft way she spoke when she was in his arms, and something about her tenderness made him bite back his discontentment.

Why not give her the benefit of the doubt? After all, *he* had been the one to bring the subject of a new wardrobe up in the first place. And she certainly hadn't been demanding that he take her to fancy and impressive places, had she? In fact, last week when he had asked her if she wanted to go along with him to meet a visiting member of the Italian government, she had blushed and said that she'd probably be in the way.

In fact, she had been right—it had not been a suitable occasion for partners. But Jessica was unusual for her gender. She didn't swoop on every opportunity to be seen with him—to make the world aware that she was the woman sharing his bed at night.

That had not been why she'd turned the invitation down, of course. It had been because she was insecure about not having the right clothes to wear. His mouth hardened. Well, not for much longer.

The car dropped them outside one of the city's swishest department stores and he led the way past the frothy rails of lingerie towards the clothing section with assistants fluttering around him like moths.

'Can I help you, sir?' questioned an elegant Frenchwoman, dressed entirely in black, who was clearly in charge of the department.

Salvatore rested his hand with lazy possession at Jessica's waist. 'I want to buy my girlfriend some clothes,' he said.

Lucky girlfriend, the Frenchwoman's eyes seemed to say. 'Is there anything in particular you're looking for, sir?'

'Everything,' he said softly.

They were taken to a private section at the back of the store, where Salvatore was given a chair and coffee while Jessica was shown into a huge changing room with horrible unflattering mirrors everywhere, and the Frenchwoman began to bring in outfit after outfit.

'Sir, he is very particular about what he likes.' The woman beamed as the zip was slid up the back of a gown of silk chiffon so fragile that Jessica wondered how it could possibly have been sewn into such a flattering shape.

'You could say that,' said Jessica, feeling rather dazed by the swift efficiency of the expedition. This was so well choreographed that it felt more like opera than shopping, and the moment where a lacy suspender belt and several pairs of fine silk stockings were added to the purchases was the moment when she really *felt* like a mistress.

It seemed like hours later that other assistants were dispatched to help load the packages in the boot of the car, with Jessica walking rather self-consciously at Salvatore's side. She was wearing some of her new clothes—a fitted day-dress in silk jersey which swirled around her knee. Underneath the whole ensemble was the most outrageously sexy underwear she had ever seen.

Her old clothes had been bundled into one of the shop's carrier bags and lay somewhere amid the new, shiny bags—all but forgotten. And Jessica couldn't quite decide whether she felt like a butterfly emerging from the chrysalis—or whether it wasn't just a little bit frightening to have cast off her old persona quite so completely.

'I'll get the car to drop you off at home,' said Salvatore, with a yawn. 'And I will see you on Wednesday.'

She couldn't help herself. He had just spent a fortune on her and yet he wasn't going to see her for four days? 'Not...not tonight?'

There was a brief silence while she looked at him in surprise and disappointment.

But Salvatore's mind was made up. He needed some space. He needed to put her into her proper place in his life and to show her that he was the boss. He closed his mind to the lure of her skimpy new garments with a hard, glimmering smile. 'No, not tonight, *cara.* I have to make a trip to Santa Barbara—didn't I mention it?'

No, he had not mentioned it—but why would he need to? Mistresses didn't qualify for any of the normal, common courtesies which existed between a man and a woman, did they?

So show a little pride, she told herself.

'I don't think you did,' she said, with a slow kind of dignity.

When the car drew up outside her house, she somehow managed to turn to him with a smile. 'Thanks for all my lovely new clothes,' she said, even though his rebuff made her want leave them all behind in his car, untouched.

But where would that get her? The proud Sicilian would only see it as an unforgivable snub to his pride and she simply wasn't prepared to risk it. Not yet.

'Have a good trip, Salvatore,' she said, and leaned over to kiss him briefly.

Her lips were cool—as cool as her attitude. He hadn't seen her like this before and, perversely, it made him want her all the more. Sensing her dismissal, he brought her closer into his body, his fingers feeling the unaccustomedly soft luxury of the silk and cashmere she now wore. Had indulging her begun to spoil her—to corrupt her in the way that new riches sometimes did? Would her sweet eagerness now be replaced by a kind of bored dissatisfaction?

He spoke against her mouth. 'Maybe I've changed my mind, *cara*,' he murmured. 'Maybe I'll take you home after all.'

His proximity enticed her as much as the sultry promise in his voice—even though it shamed her to admit it. But Jessica recognised that something far more important than desire lay at stake here. Being a mistress was one thing and of course that inevitably meant she would be at Salvatore's beck and call.

But allowing him to move her around as if she were some little pawn in a game of chess he wasn't particularly interested in playing—well, that was something else. First he pushed her away and then he pulled her back—and she was supposed to just fall in with his every whim? His allure was powerful, but how would she feel if she allowed him to turn the car round and drive back to Chelsea, leaving her lying there in the morning feeling somehow *used*?

'You have to get ready for your trip,' she said demurely, drawing away from him and seeing his eyes narrow.

Salvatore studied her, watching as she picked up her bag—a new squashy crescent of a thing which matched the sexy boots she wore. Money gave a person power, he recognised. Put his sweet little cleaner in costly clothes and she could be as much of a diva as the next woman.

Should he insist that she bow to his will? he wondered idly. Kiss her until she complied? But he could see the fierce look of pride which had darkened her grey eyes and made them look positively stormy, and he sighed.

Let her enjoy her pointless little victory. One day he would be gone and she would ask herself how she could have possibly turned down a night with him.

'I'll see you next week,' he drawled softly.

CHAPTER ELEVEN

THE doorbell pealed loudly an hour before it was supposed to and Jessica looked at her half-dressed figure in horror. He was early—and Salvatore was *never* early!

Hanging on the front of her wardrobe was a floor-length gown of white silk-satin so beautiful that she was almost scared to put it on. Salvatore was driving straight from the airport to pick her up and not only had she been ticking off the seconds since he'd been away—but she had wanted to look her very best.

It had been a horrible week. She'd regretted her decision to let pride stop her from spending that last night with him and she had begun to realise just how dull her jobs were. It was as if every time Salvatore went away his absence threw a spotlight on her life and emphasised all its deficiencies. And that wasn't a very positive aspect of the relationship either, was it?

Pulling the soft silk-satin over her head, Jessica strained her ears for the sound of his deep baritone but heard nothing—until there was a tap on her door and she opened it to find Freya standing there.

'You've got to come and sign for a parcel,' she said, her voice growing wistful. 'And that's the most gorgeous dress I've ever seen, Jessica.'

'A parcel?' said Jessica distractedly, smoothing the delicate fabric over her hips and walking rather self-consciously into the hall, where Willow was chatting to the delivery man.

After she'd signed for it, her two housemates crowded round her and for some reason Jessica's fingers were trembling as she slit open the padded envelope containing a small box. Was that because there was only one person who would send her a package by special delivery?

'It's a box,' she said.

'We can see that for ourselves, stupid—go on, open it!'

She untied the dark green grosgrain ribbon and flipped open the lid of the box and the three of them gasped in shocked unison.

'Oh, my word!'

'Jessica!'

Jessica swallowed. 'There must be some kind of mistake.'

'Read the card and see what it says.'

Her fingers were trembling as she pulled the card out of the accompanying envelope. 'I couldn't find stones to match your eyes,' it read, 'but these should go with most things.' She stared at the brilliant circlet of diamonds and swallowed. 'They can't possibly be real.'

Willow snatched the bracelet out of the box and held it up to the light with the skill of a prospector. 'Oh, they're real all right. My word, Jessica—what on earth did you do to make him buy you these?'

Jessica flinched, taking the bracelet back, even though the cold and beautiful stones now felt somehow tainted by Willow's words. But hadn't she been wondering the same thing herself?

Freya was staring at them curiously. 'They must be worth an absolute fortune,' she said. 'Better put them on your insurance.'

'But I haven't got any insurance!'

'It's about time you did—particularly if there's going to be more of this kind of thing arriving.'

Jessica slid the bracelet on and stared at it as it caught and reflected the light. It was beautiful. Utterly beautiful—but she found herself wondering why had he bought it for her—apart from presumably wanting her to wear it this evening. A suitable and costly accompaniment to an expensive dress.

Her heart lurched from the ever-present fear which was never too far away. Or was it a goodbye gift? Quickly, she took it off and put it back in the box just as the doorbell rang.

'He usually sends his driver,' confided Willow as Jessica slipped the box in her bag and picked up her wrap and the overnight bag which contained her work clothes and toothbrush.

But tonight he hadn't sent the driver. Salvatore stood there on her doorstep, looking more gorgeous than Jessica could ever remember.

He was dressed in a formal black dinner jacket and

bow tie, the suit emphasising his height—the powerful thrust of his thighs and the broad shoulders. Freya had never met him before and as Jessica introduced him she registered her housemate's dazed expression. And hadn't Jessica felt much the same way herself, the first time she'd ever run across him? Didn't she feel a little like that now, as if this were all some kind of dream which would soon evaporate?

Salvatore's eyes swept over her. The pure white satin coated her curves like cream, giving her an expensive and almost unrecognisable look. He felt the flicker of a pulse. This was a Jessica he had never seen before—a Jessica he had helped create with his money.

'You look beautiful, *cara*,' he said softly, once they were in the car. 'But why aren't you wearing my bracelet?'

Jessica knew she would never be beautiful, but she was aware that the white dress seemed to do remarkable things to her figure. She took the box from her bag and opened it.

'*This* is beautiful,' she said quietly. 'Is it on loan?'

He looked surprised. 'Of course it's not. It is a gift—from me, to you. Put it on.'

'But it's not my birthday, Salvatore—and even if it was, I couldn't possibly accept something as valuable as this. Thank you, but no thanks.'

He searched her face. Another game? The refusal of a gift with the intention of making him believe she was uninterested in his money? Knowing, of course, that such a proud gesture would guarantee the purchase of an even more expensive trinket. But Jessica's expression was set and determined, and there was a defiant look of pride flashing from her grey eyes.

'I don't want your refusal. I want you to wear it tonight,' he said softly as he lifted the bracelet from its velvet base.

'But it's not—'

'No buts. *No*. Listen to me, Jessica. I am a wealthy man—and it pleases me to buy you diamonds.' His eyes gleamed at her. 'Surely you would not deny your Salvatore such simple pleasure as that?'

She tried to tell herself fiercely that the *your* Salvatore was simply a slip of the tongue. He wasn't *her* Salvatore any more than she was *his* Jessica. But he was managing to make her refusal seem crazy and wasn't there a tiny voice in her head urging her to accept the gift? Wasn't she discovering that she rather *liked* the costly gems—and wasn't that a rather inadvisable and dangerous liking to acquire, given her circumstances?

'I suppose…if you put it like that.'

He smiled as he sensed her capitulation and began to slide the glittering bangle over her tiny wrist. Didn't they say that every woman had her price?

'Wear it for me, and then kiss me and tell me how much you have missed me.'

Her lips brushed against his. 'I've missed you,' she whispered truthfully.

But her head was spinning as they kissed. She felt as if she had put herself in some kind of catch-22 situation—unable to refuse his gift, but her acceptance of it making her feel as if she had crossed some invisible line and sold out in some way.

And suddenly she saw with remarkable clarity what she had become. She was there to warm his bed when he desired her and to be kitted out with costly clothes and expensive pieces of jewellery which were supposed to make her look like she belonged to his world when she did not. And she never would. She was nothing but an imposter. A cleaner masquerading as the legitimate partner of a billionaire. A cleaner who had fallen in love with him somewhere along the way.

Suddenly the bangle felt as cold and heavy as her heart, a manacle which hung around her slender wrist. I've fallen in love with him, she realised, and a terrible hopelessness clenched at her heart.

'You are cold?' Salvatore questioned as he felt her tremble in a way that was more frozen than desire.

'A little.' She pulled the stole closer around her bare shoulders. 'There isn't very much to this dress.'

'Which happens to be its appeal,' he commented drily as the car drew up directly outside the Natural History Museum.

Jessica looked startled as she stared up at the huge building, where her grandmother had once brought her during one of the school holidays. 'Don't tell me we're eating dinner in *here*?' she questioned nervously.

'We are. It is often hired out for charity and corporate events.'

Inside, the place had been transformed with glamour on a scale Jessica hadn't believed existed. Tight scarlet roses were bunched into tall, dark vases which were placed everywhere and starlike lights twinkled against an indigo backdrop. Crystal laid tables were dotted beneath the impressive form of a giant dinosaur, which towered over the evening's proceedings.

But tonight Jessica couldn't seem to get rid of the gnawing sensation that she had no real place here. That in Salvatore's car was her overnight bag with her neat office clothes, which were a world away from the slippery silk-satin she was wearing.

Their table was right at the top of the room and, in the dazzle of introductions made, a wiry, red-headed man she half recognised shook Salvatore by the hand.

'I didn't expect to see you again so soon!' he exclaimed, and then appeared to notice Jessica. 'Salvatore and I bumped into each other in Santa Barbara earlier in the week,' he explained as they took their seats, and then added, 'Hi, nice to meet you. I'm Jeremy, by the way.'

Jessica nodded as it all came back, remembering the keen fisherman who had been so kind to her on that first, rather nerve-racking evening when she'd been Salvatore's pretend date at the dinner party. And an unexpected feeling of relief washed over her. She actually *knew* someone here! Already she had a bit of a history with Salvatore, despite all her fretting. Maybe she could fit in, after all.

'We've met before,' she said, with a smile. 'I'm Jessica. Remember?'

Jeremy's eyes remained blank. 'I don't think…'

'At that lovely house in Kensington. Garth and Amy's.'

Jeremy's eyes cleared, but his look of comprehension was quickly replaced by one of confusion. 'Yes, of course. You asked me about fishing. But what has happened to you?'

Jessica gave a look of mock-surprise. 'What do you mean?'

He shook his head. 'Oh, nothing. Silly mistake.'

'Please.' She lowered her voice. 'What do you mean?'

He gave her an odd kind of smile. 'Just that you used to look so…different.' He cleared his throat as he reached for his wine glass in a gesture which was unmistakably intended to close the subject. 'That really is a magnificent bracelet you're wearing.'

Jessica went through the motions of eating the meal, but inside her stomach felt as if it had been turned into a tight steel drum. Despite his best diplomatic attempts, Jeremy couldn't have made it plainer if he'd tried. The woman he'd met that night—the one he'd clearly liked and enjoyed talking to—had vanished.

And in her place was a new woman—one created for and by Salvatore. Clothed in white silk-satin and dripping in diamonds, she had been transformed. All traces of the real Jessica ironed away to enable her to become the stereotypical mistress.

Somehow she managed to endure the endless courses and then an auction for which it seemed that Salvatore had donated the top bid of an all-expenses holiday in a luxury Sicilian villa. Images of the island were flashed up on a giant screen—a place of seemingly unimaginable beauty with its lemon trees lining amazing beaches, exquisite old towns and dark green mountains.

Jessica stole a glance at his profile, seeing the faint

smile which curved the edges of his lips as the slide-show finished.

Was he imagining his permanent return to his island home, and the day when he married his virgin bride? A pang ripped through her, and as they were leaving she found herself wondering if he would ever remember Jessica Martin—or whether she was just one in a long line of anonymous mistresses, all interchangeable in their costly clothes and jewels.

Laden with designer goodie-bags, they stepped into the waiting limousine and as the car purred away Salvatore turned to her.

'You were very quiet tonight, Jessica.'

'Was I?'

'Any particular reason?'

She looked out of the window, at the glittering night which was flashing by. 'Not really.'

'You were perhaps a little disappointed that Jeremy was less amenable to your charms than last time?' he questioned.

He was more perceptive than she sometimes gave him credit for, but of course he had completely missed the point. 'He didn't recognise me,' she said.

He stroked the silk of her gown reflectively. 'But that is a good thing, surely? Isn't the whole idea of a brand-new wardrobe to give the wearer a brand-new look?'

'Is it?' She felt like a flower plucked from a simple country garden who had changed into a forced, hothouse bloom and left without fragrance or freshness.

'Of course it is,' he said softly. 'It would be naïve to expect your experience with me not to leave its mark on you, Jessica.'

She felt as if she'd sold out to his money and that Jeremy had noticed and disapproved of it in some way—but what was the point in telling Salvatore that? He was just back from a long trip. He didn't want to hear about her crushing insecurity—it wasn't actually going to *change* anything. Mistresses weren't supposed to become emotionally involved, were they? That was the number one rule. And I've broken it, she thought unhappily as she turned to stare into his handsome face. I've broken it big time.

'Oh, it would have been nice to have been alone with you,' she said instead.

'*Nice*, Jessica?' he mocked as he pulled her into his arms. 'What have I told you before about lacklustre words which say nothing?' He put his mouth close to hers. 'Come on, think of a more accurate description, *mia tesoro*.'

Jessica closed her eyes and swallowed. This was easy. Too easy. 'Incredible. It would have been incredible to have had you all to myself,' she whispered. 'Is that better?'

He touched her breast. 'Much better.'

'And...how was Santa Barbara?'

'Oh, cold. Busy. Predictable.' And filled with glamorous women, it seemed—most of whom had wasted no time in letting him know that a Sicilian billionaire was very desirable indeed.

But, inexplicably, he had missed Jessica, despite her stubbornness just before he'd left. Not just the sex—because he always enjoyed sex with the appetite of a man who enjoyed food when his belly was empty, or fine wine when he wanted the luxury of relaxation.

He had missed the ease he enjoyed with her. Her ability to listen to him and her refusal to say what was expected of her, simply because of her inferior social position. He had felt her absence keenly and that had alerted him to danger. Because missing someone meant that you were in some way dependent on them—and he was dependent on no one. He ran the flat of his hand against the silky surface of her hair. 'Have you missed me?' he questioned idly.

'Yes.'

'How much?'

She wanted to cling to him, to shower every inch of his autocratic face with soft, butterfly kisses—hug him with a poignant and heartfelt embrace for what could never be. But mistresses didn't do that, either. He had bought her the dress and the diamonds—she knew exactly what was expected of her. Instead, she trickled her fingernails over one taut thigh and heard him groan. 'This much.'

'Do that some more,' he urged softly. 'Ah, *sì*.'

They barely made it in through the front door. Their hands and lips were frantic—with Salvatore removing the white satin from Jessica's trembling body with the dexterity of a man peeling a banana.

He took her against the wall—wild and urgent—her gasping cries inciting him as he drove into her.

But afterwards, Jessica felt shaken, not just by that stormy coming together, but by the certain knowledge of how much she was going to miss him.

They barely slept at all. She wondered if it was absence which made the sex seem much more intense than usual. As if it had moved on to a different dimension. Or was that simply wishful thinking on her part? A woman conjuring up a fantasy because she had fallen in love with a man who was out of bounds. Well, falling in love with Salvatore was about as sensible as diving into the sea from a cliff-top when you could barely swim. And he had warned her that this was going nowhere—so there was no one to blame but herself.

Next morning, she slipped quietly from the bed into the shower so as not to wake him, but when she returned to the bedroom to put on her office clothes she found him staring at her.

'That was some night,' he observed softly.

Jessica swallowed. 'Yes.'

The blue gaze didn't waver. 'Let's do it again tonight. I have an early evening meeting out by the river—come with me, and we'll have dinner together afterwards. We could stay over if you like—there's a beautiful hotel.' He smiled. 'Wake up in the morning in the countryside for a change.'

'Salvatore, I can't—'

His invitation had been impromptu but her ready refusal irritated him. 'Can't?'

'No. I'm sorry. It's too short notice.'

Suddenly he felt angry, with her and with himself, and he couldn't work out why. He leaned back against the pillows, his dark features assuming a bored expression. 'Jessica—I thought we'd already established the ground rules. We're way past that stage, *cara.* And if you think that refusing me like a sixteen-year-old virgin is going to make you more desirable, then I am afraid that you are very much mistaken.'

Jessica froze. Not only had he forgotten—and dismissed—her *real* life, the one which involved regular work for a regular wage-packet to pay her rent, but he had turned round and accused her of emotional manipulation. And it hurt. Hadn't he learned *anything* about her in the time they'd been together? No, of course he hadn't. He wasn't interested in finding out anything about her as a woman—that kind of knowledge didn't even register on his radar.

Just because he had made love to her with such passion during the night didn't actually *mean* anything, did it? The supposedly tender way he had held her had nothing to do with emotion. Because Salvatore hadn't changed. Nothing had changed—except maybe *her* feelings.

So stop it right now. Remind him of the reality.

'I've got my job to do tonight,' she said quietly. 'Cleaning in your office. Remember that, Salvatore? It happens to be how we met.'

There was a pause. 'Well, I'm absolving you of the responsibility. Leave it. Don't do it. For heaven's sake—you can easily miss a night.'

'I can't do that.'

'You can and you will. I'm the chairman of the damned company, Jessica—and what I say goes!'

She shook her head, clinging onto this last piece of independence like a drowning woman scrabbling at a slippery rock. 'But I don't work for *you*, Salvatore. I work for Top Kleen who won't be very happy if I make a habit of missing work. For a start they might begin to wonder *why* I've been given the evening off by the boss—and we wouldn't want them knowing that, would we? And then…' She paused, before drawing a deep breath. Remind him of the reality.

'Then there's the money,' she finished painfully. 'I need that money, Salvatore—that's why I do the job.'

Salvatore smiled. This was language he could understand. Reaching for his wallet, he pulled out a thick wad of notes and peeled off several before holding them up. 'How much do you need?' he questioned carelessly.

Jessica's cheeks stained with anger and embarrassment. 'That wasn't what I meant at all. I don't want your money.'

'Oh, for goodness sake—it's no big deal,' he snapped. 'I want your company. I don't want you cleaning my office. Surely if you take emotion out of the situation, you can see the logic in my offer? It makes perfect sense. I have more than enough and you don't. So take the damned money, Jessica.'

She shook her head.

'Please, Jessica.'

It was the 'please' that did it. Who could deny

Salvatore when he asked her like that? Reluctantly, Jessica nodded.

'You'll take it?'

The truth was that she *could* see the logic in his words—but that didn't stop the feeling of shame which washed over her. Knowing she was trapped. Knowing that there was no other solution than to accept an offer which he didn't even realise was so insulting.

'Yes, I'll take it.'

With trembling fingers she walked towards him and removed two of the notes, shaking her head when he extended the pile towards her again. She would take exactly what she would have earned, and no more.

'Jessica—'

'I'll see you later,' she said quietly, and, bending to plant a swift kiss on his lips, she turned and left.

Outside, it was raining but Jessica barely noticed the bus which splashed icy water over her legs. She bought a cup of coffee from the office vending machine, which tasted pretty disgusting, but at least it was hot.

Forcing herself to try to concentrate, she sat down at her desk to survey the mass of emails which had accumulated, but she had only been working for a couple of minutes when the phone rang.

It was the hospital—and the call that she took seemed to put all her problems into perspective.

CHAPTER TWELVE

'YOUR grandmother's going to be fine, Miss Martin—it's the shock as much as anything.'

Jessica nodded, her eyes filling with tears as she clutched at her grandmother's hand, thinking how unbelievably pale and small she looked lying in the hospital bed. But she supposed that was what happened when someone you'd thought of as indestructible all their lives managed to injure themselves. For the first time she realised that her grandmother was getting old. That nothing ever remained the same.

She looked up at the orthopaedic surgeon. 'Thank you so much, Doctor. I really appreciate it.'

'She's a very interesting patient,' he said, giving a quick smile.

After the surgeon had left, Jessica turned to her grandmother with a mixture of love and exasperation. 'But you shouldn't have *been* dancing the salsa!' she exclaimed. 'Not at your age!'

Her grandmother smiled. 'Oh, rubbish, Jessica. There's far too much of "don't do this" and "don't do that" once you pass sixty. I've always enjoyed dancing, as well you know—it was that clod of a partner who made me fall.' She held up her wrist, which was covered in a bright pink plaster, and pulled a face. 'The trouble is that it's my right wrist. So no lifting. No carrying. I'm going to have to get someone to do my shopping.'

Jessica nodded, her mind spinning. 'And someone to do the cleaning,' she pointed out as she picked over the possibilities of how she could possibly help. She could stay here tonight, of course; she'd have to. She'd already rung a rather distracted Salvatore, interrupting him at the office, which was something she'd never done before, and told him she'd be staying away.

'What's happened?' he demanded.

'Oh, my grandmother took a tumble. She's broken her wrist, but is fine otherwise.'

'That's good,' he said distractedly, but Jessica could hear the sound of a telephone ringing and the low hum of voices in the background and knew that he wasn't really interested in the fine print of her family troubles.

And work wouldn't give her indefinite leave to look after her grandmother—why, they'd only let a girl from the finance department have two days off to fly to Ireland when her father had died.

'We need to get someone to come in and help you,' she said slowly. 'There's that agency in the next town, of course.'

A look of concern crossed her grandmother's face. 'But they're expensive, Jessica—everyone says so, and we haven't got—'

'Oh, yes, we have—and you're not to worry about a thing. Not a thing,' Jessica told the old lady fiercely. 'I can sort something out.'

Jessica knew exactly what she was going to do, even though the thought of it was daunting. She had the bracelet in her handbag—she kept it close to her at all times, terrified to leave something so precious in the house. Yet, in a funny kind of way, the thought of getting rid of it was a relief. It represented both too much and yet nothing at all. It had not been given as a token of love, but as a token of worth. Its price was its value—so why should she hang onto it when it just taunted her of what she would never have from Salvatore?

The sum which the jeweller offered sounded ridiculously high. 'This is a simply fabulous piece,' he breathed as he stared at it for ages through his eyeglass.

He seemed surprised when Jessica accepted the price he offered without demur—but what did she know about diamond prices in the current market? She needed money, and quickly. And for once local hearsay hadn't been exaggerated—the agency she was drafting in to help really was expensive.

'I've arranged for someone to come in twice a day to help you,' she told her grandmother once they were back in the tiny cottage where Jessica had spent most of her childhood. 'Someone who'll do any washing, or cooking or shopping. Whatever you like, really—you just have to tell them.'

'Gosh—I'll have to fracture my wrist more often.'

'Just you dare!'

Jessica was exhausted. It felt strange to sleep in her little bed that night, in the back bedroom which overlooked the apple trees. The skies were pitch black and lit only by starlight, and a car-less hush settled over the place once the only pub had shut, cloaking it in a comforting kind of silence. A village which had always seemed frighteningly quiet and lacking in any kind of life now seemed to offer a soothing balm to her troubled thoughts.

Jessica woke up next morning to the sound of birdsong, and she lay there wondering whether she had done the right thing in going up to London to try to make something of herself. Had her ambition overreached itself? True, she'd ended up living in an okay house with the very real chance of promotion in her office job. And, yes, she happened to have an amazing lover—but that bit was only temporary, and she was having to work round the clock for the rest.

She left her grandmother playing a slow game of one-handed poker-dice with an elderly neighbour and then headed back to London, where she was back at her desk by lunchtime.

From time to time she glanced down at the handbag by her feet, knowing that she needed to bank the thick wad of cash which the jeweller had given her. And surely she needed to tell Salvatore what she had done?

Jessica bit her lip.

How could she? Wouldn't that essentially be saying to him that she needed his expensive presents to support her lifestyle? And mightn't it look as if she were hinting for more?

After all, Salvatore didn't care whether she actually *wore* the jewels—it was the gesture of giving them which counted, and clearly giving diamonds to your mistress was de rigeur.

But later that evening she flew into his arms as if she had been separated from him for a year, rather than an unexpected night, and he laughed softly as he kissed her.

'Missed me?'

'Yes.'

'How is your grandmother?'

'She's fine.'

He took her on an overnight trip to Paris, where they stayed in an amazing hotel on the Place de la Concorde. They bought frothy lingerie in a little shop on the Avenue Montaigne and Jessica insisted on taking a boat ride down the Seine. Salvatore laughed and accused her of making him feel like a tourist.

'But we *are* tourists!' she retorted. 'And, besides, I've never seen you looking quite so relaxed before.'

It was true, he thought as they queued for tickets at the Musée d'Orsay. He hadn't stood in a queue for years—and for once in his life he felt utterly free.

He found himself watching her as they strolled around the famous Flea Market. Left to her own devices, Jessica seemed to like pottering among the junk, lifting a perfect moonstone on a silver chain which had caught her eye and holding it to the light.

'Look, it's the *exact* colour of the Seine,' she observed.

Salvatore frowned. Was she hinting for another

present? But surely not something as commonplace as that cheap little necklace?

'Where's your bracelet?' he questioned later, over lunch—as he trickled raspberry vinegar onto an oyster and held it in front of her lips.

Jessica froze as obligation hovered over her—but how could she possibly destroy this perfect moment with such mundane reality? 'I've…I've left it at home,' she lied as he slid the oyster into her mouth.

On Monday she gave into sweet pressure and again cancelled her cleaning job so that Salvatore could take her to the Festival Hall to listen to a visiting violinist who tore at her heartstrings.

On Tuesday, she dashed up after work to see her grandmother, who, it seemed, was quickly becoming used to her new leisurely life and the fuss being made of her.

On Wednesday she deliberately turned up late at Cardini's—because Salvatore had told her he was having a meeting which might run over and she couldn't face turning up in front of him and all his colleagues in her pink overall and scarf. And as she'd told herself time and time again—as long as she did the work, then no one was any the wiser if she ran over her appointed hours.

But when she walked into his office it was not empty, as she had expected. And there was no sign of her Sicilian lover. Instead, her supervisor was waiting there for her.

'Perhaps you'd like to explain yourself,' said the woman grimly.

There was no explanation which would satisfy even the most reasonable of people, and, judging by the look of simmering rage on the face of the supervisor, reasonable was the last thing she was feeling. It seemed that a whole catalogue of complaints about Jessica's behaviour had been building up.

'It's gone round the building like wildfire!' the woman began, her words barely coherent as they poured out in a torrent of venom. 'A member of Top Kleen having an affair with the company chairman. I've never heard anything like it!'

Some rogue instinct made Jessica want to retort that it said a lot for the calibre of Top Kleen employees that the boss should *want* to have an affair with one of its employees at all! But she could see that such a remark would inflame an already inflammatory situation and half an hour later she was leaving the building with Salvatore's car on its way to fetch her.

For a moment she wanted to laugh at the irony of the sacked cleaner being collected by the boss's limousine, and the next she was slumped in the back seat, speeding towards Chelsea and feeling as if her life were being slowly dismantled, piece by piece.

Salvatore was talking on the phone when he answered the door to her, and waved her in the direction of the drinks tray. All Jessica wanted to do was to hug him, to wrap her arms tightly around his neck and have a little moan about her job and the aggressive supervisor. But comfort was not part of his role, just as seeking emotional reassurance was not part of hers.

So she hung up her coat and poured herself a drink and waited until he finished the call.

He looked up at her. *'Ciao, bella,'* he said softly.

'Important?' asked Jessica automatically, for she had noticed him frown.

'Just a deal in the Far East which is worth looking at. You remember the hotel on Phuket I was telling you about? Well, one of my cousins—Giacomo—is thinking of buying it. But I think the price is too high and the trouble is that he is hot-headed and impulsive.' His gaze swept over her. 'I was wondering why you wanted the car to collect you so early and how pale you looked,' he said softly. 'Are you ill, *cara*?'

Jessica swallowed, the term of endearment spoken in that deceptively gentle tone making her feel even more wobbly than she already did. 'No, I'm not ill. I've been sacked, actually. Sacked from my cleaning job,' she elaborated.

The frown deepened. 'For what, precisely?'

The laugh she attempted fell flat. 'Unprofessional behaviour is the phrase they used. Somehow my agency have found out that I've been…that we've been… They know about us, Salvatore,' she said, aware even as she said it that there was no *us*. 'They think that my affair with you has made me abuse my position, and in a way they have a point. I'm sorry if your reputation is going to suffer as a consequence of that.'

There was a pause. 'You think that anything would reflect badly on *my* reputation?' he challenged softly. 'Or that I seek the good opinion of others through the way I live my life?' His blue eyes hardened into chips of sapphire as he walked towards her. 'And you want to know something? I am glad that you have lost that stupid job, Jessica—it ate into too much of your time. Time you should have been spending with me.'

Jessica looked at him incredulously. Now he had dismissed a chunk of her life as if it were of no consequence! 'Of course it did—it was a *job*! I wasn't doing it for fun, you know.'

'I know that. You were doing it for money—but money is not a problem, is it, *cara*?' he questioned silkily, and pulled her into his arms. 'Since I have more than enough to go round. I thought that we established that the other day. So can we please stop pretending and just accept that?'

Of course she was tempted. Who wouldn't have been—especially when he was touching her like that and his breath was warm against her cheek? But something prevented Jessica from taking the easy way out that he was offering her. She remembered how cheap she'd felt as he had peeled those notes from his wallet. She thought of the costly diamond bracelet now languishing in the jeweller's and the lie she had told him about it, because she had panicked in Paris. And because you knew he'd go crazy if you told him the truth.

Jessica bit her lip. 'I'm not taking any more money from you,' she said. 'I've taken enough.'

'But I insist.'

'You can insist all you want, Salvatore—but I'm not accepting it.'

He studied her for a moment, but could see she meant it. And although it riled him to have his wishes thwarted—wasn't it admirable in a way that she had turned down his offer? She was a stubborn, sometimes proud woman, he thought, a reluctant smile curving his lips. Even though it was futile, he rather liked her determination to maintain her independence—it was almost worth the occasional disruption to his social life. But enough was enough. She had made her point and now he would make his.

He lifted her chin, fixing her in the blaze from his eyes. 'Refuse my money if you must,' he said softly. 'But I don't want you getting another part-time job—not while you are with me. Is that understood?'

How formidable he sounded in that moment, she thought. Some rebel streak urged her to tell him that he had no right to dictate the terms of her life. Yet as Jessica gazed up into the unyielding glint in his eyes she registered that maybe he did. Because wasn't another function of the mistress to be always available? Not to have to turn down your lover because you had to rush off to clean and polish.

She laid her head against his shoulders and closed her eyes and suddenly she didn't care if he was dictating terms or not. Because this was where she most wanted to be—in his arms. These precious moments which were ticking away all too quickly.

Surely it *was* slightly crazy for her to be cleaning offices—forcing her to cancel dates and leave her billionaire lover cooling his heels. And surely she *could* manage without an additional job—at least until the affair finished.

'Is it, Jessica?' he repeated silkily.

How could she resist him anything? Snuggling into his hard body with a sigh, she turned her face upwards and gave a little shrug of her shoulders. 'Okay, then,' she agreed softly. 'Just this once, I'll let you insist.'

But as Salvatore looked down at her, a strange kind of feeling twisted in his gut. All he was aware of was the quiet grey light from her eyes, the pale oval of her face and the petal-pink lips. As those lips parted unfamiliar feelings began to tug at his senses and in that moment he felt completely perplexed.

He shook his head—as if he could shake away the sensations which were creeping over him like unwelcome intruders. He didn't want to *feel*—and certainly not with her. Not until he had decided the time was right and the woman was right—and this woman most emphatically was not.

His mouth hardened. 'I'm glad that's been sorted out,' he purred. 'From now on, you'll be available when I need you. Understood?'

Jessica nodded, telling herself that his use of the word 'available' didn't exactly boost her self-confidence. 'I just wish I could contribute a bit more.'

The twist in his gut became something much more recognisable. 'Oh, but you do,' he said unsteadily, his hands roving over her bottom and beginning to ruck up her skirt. He felt her thighs begin to quiver coolly beneath the hot, seeking heat of his fingers. 'You contribute in the most imaginative way of all, *cara mia*.'

'Salvatore!' she gasped, but her desire was overshadowed by the harsh truth of his words. That sex was her contribution—and that was all he wanted. All he needed—certainly from her. So you'd better start dismantling your fantasies before they get too real, she told herself fiercely, and gave herself up to the plunder of his kiss.

He took her to bed and that night Salvatore dreamt of Sicily, wondering if it was some kind of portent. Were his dreams trying to tell him that his time in England was finished? That maybe he should return to the island of his birth and begin to search for a woman to bear his sons, as he had always intended to do?

The figure beside him stirred lazily. 'Can't you sleep?' she murmured, her hands reaching up automatically to caress his shoulders, the tight muscles relaxing beneath the ministrations of her touch.

'No.'

'Can I help?'

'You can try.' And he made a sound between a laugh and a moan as she began to touch him.

This time the pleasure was stealthy, but the power of his orgasm took him by surprise. How the hell could someone so inexperienced be so good? Because she's passionate, that's why, he told himself.

His thoughts were troubled even as his eyelids began drifting to a close. Tomorrow, he would speak to his cousin, Vincenzo, and discuss returning to Sicily—and in the meantime he would buy Jessica another piece of jewellery. Something bigger this time. It would perhaps make up for the indignity of being sacked because of her relationship with him.

Something to remember him by.

Next day, once his assistant had gone home and the building was quiet, he clicked onto the website of the leading diamond retailer. He liked diamonds—their purity and glittering beauty—and they were always a good investment.

Idly, he scrolled down through the blur of dazzling gemstones until his attention was caught by the unexpected. Eyes narrowing, he returned to the page with a growing sense of disbelief as he began to study the photograph carefully.

There could be no mistake.

He felt the harsh beat of his heart. He tasted the stale flavour of disappointment—but, beneath it all, he was aware of the sensation of having been thrown a lifeline. Something which dissolved all his niggling doubts in an instant. He smiled, but it was a hard, cruel smile. Because this was something he understood almost better than anything. She was nothing but a cheap little gold-digger, after all.

Picking up the phone, he punched out her number. 'Jessica?' he questioned. 'Can you get over to the apartment right away?'

CHAPTER THIRTEEN

JESSICA arrived in a rush. It had been raining outside and her hair was spattered with raindrops which glittered on her shiny head. Like jewels, Salvatore thought grimly. She was wearing a cute coat, a leather trench which clung to her curves and gave her an expensive, pampered look—a look which she wore like a second skin.

How quickly his cleaner lover had adapted to luxury, he marvelled. Salvatore's mouth hardened as she removed the coat to reveal a slither of silk jersey beneath. And pale stocking and killer heels. A pulse began to beat at his temple. She looked like what she'd become—a rich man's plaything. He wondered how she was going to take it when she heard that he would no longer be bankrolling her. That the presents were stopping and so was the lifestyle.

But he would give her one last chance to redeem herself.

'You look beautiful,' he said softly as he hung the coat for her and gestured for her to follow him into the sitting room.

'Do I?' Jessica was trying to get better at receiving compliments—and, to be honest, it was getting easier all the time because Salvatore made her *feel* beautiful. Sometimes, when he was running his hands over her body in bed, stroking her as if she were some sleek racehorse—she felt as good as anybody else. 'Why, thank you,' she said softly and looked at him expectantly. 'Is everything okay? You sounded…I don't know…*urgent* on the phone.'

'Did I? Sit down. Like a drink?'

She shook her head. 'No. No, thanks.'

His gaze flicked over her. 'That outfit looks wonderful, *cara*—but it is a little on the plain side.'

'You think so?'

'I think it could do with a little embellishment, that's all. Why do you never wear that diamond bracelet I bought you? Does it not please you?'

Jessica gave a high little laugh. She had tried to forget all about the wretched bracelet—forced it to the back of her mind so that the thought of what she'd done couldn't haunt her. Because not only had she told a lie—how on earth would it look if she told him that she'd sold it? No matter how worthy the cause—wouldn't that make her look as if she were just out for everything she could get out of him?

'Oh, I…I love it,' she said, and bit her lip. 'In fact, I love it so much that I've put it somewhere safe—and you know what sometimes happens when you do that?' She met the cool expression in his eyes. 'What would you say if I told you I couldn't find it?'

There was a loaded pause while fury erupted within him like a dark, poisonous storm. 'I'd say you were a damned liar and a cheat!' he bit out, unable to keep up the pretence for a moment longer. He saw the alarm which had widened her grey eyes and the stain which pinkened her pale cheeks. Guilty, he thought grimly. Guilty as hell. 'And a stupid little fool to underestimate a man like me!'

'You mean…you've found out?' she breathed.

'That you flogged my gift to you at the first opportunity?' he snarled. 'Yes, I found out, Jessica. Didn't you realise that a piece of that quality would always find its way to the best dealer? How much did you get for it?'

Jessica felt sick. 'Salvatore, please…'

'Oh, please don't act as if the very mention of money is distasteful to you when clearly this was nothing but a *transaction* you were intending to capitalise on from the very beginning! Come on—how much? Nine? Ten?'

Miserably, she shook her head.

'More?'

'No. Half that, in fact.'

His eyes glittered. 'So not only have you sold it—but you've been ripped off into the bargain?' He gave a humourless laugh. 'Clearly you've never done this kind of thing before—'

'Of course I haven't!'

But deep down he knew that there was no *of course* about it. This was Salvatore on familiar and oddly comforting ground—probing with accuracy to try to find an ulterior motive. Because there was always one of those.

Riches and power attracted people who had an eye for the main chance—who wanted something for very little—and *his* big mistake had been in thinking that Jessica was any different from all the rest. He thought how very clever she'd been—at first trying to refuse the gift. All that coy reluctance about letting him pay her not to work. So simple and so clever, and yet he had been sucked right in, thinking her both stubborn and yet charmingly lacking in materialism.

'So why did you do it?' he questioned, almost conversationally. 'Go on, tell me. I'm intrigued.'

She met the resigned expression on his face and somehow that hurt even more than the fierce accusation of earlier—as if he had been expecting something like this all along. It cut right through her so that she had to blink to hold back the tears of remorse. Part of her wanted to tell him to go to hell, and to think the worst of her. Because that was what he wanted to do, she recognised suddenly.

That was the image which would fit in with Salvatore's stark vision of the world and of women in particular—that only virgins were worth marrying and all other women were gold-digging, greedy little tramps!

Well, whatever else came out of this sorry mess, he would know that she *wasn't* one of those women.

'I sold it to pay for my grandmother to have help while her broken wrist was mending!'

He gave a soft, disbelieving laugh. 'Ah, *sweet*! Like Little Red Riding Hood, perhaps?' he questioned with silky cynicism. 'Stealing through the forest with your basket of food for grandmamma? Aren't you a little too old to expect me to believe in fairy tales?'

Jessica stared at him, shaking her head in disbelief. How could she have deluded herself into believing that she loved a man with as warped a view of life as his? 'My goodness,' she breathed. 'It's never occurred to me before. It can't be easy being Salvatore Cardini, can it? Not when all the riches and power in the world can't change a fundamental mistrust in human nature!'

'A mistrust which you have just proved is well founded!' he iced out. 'If you wanted to help your grandmother, then why the hell didn't you tell me? Why didn't you come to me and explain what had happened? Am I such an ogre that you would not dare to do that, Jessica?

'Why?' he persisted. 'When that is what a woman would normally do.'

'So I'm damned if I do, and damned if I don't? I thought you were fed up with the fact that people always wanted something from you! That's the main reason I didn't ask you,' she said, her voice shaking with rage and hurt as she stared at him.

'But, according to you, I'm a gold-digger whichever way you want to look at it, aren't I, Salvatore? You forced me to take a bracelet I didn't particularly want—presumably because it satisfies some sort of mistress "code". I didn't realise that it came with certain specifications of what I was or wasn't allowed to do with it! I suppose if you'd given me perfume you would have included a list of times when I was allowed to spray it!'

'But we are having a relationship,' he snarled, 'which surely entitles you to ask for my help with your family.'

'Entitlement?' Jessica might have laughed if she hadn't been so angry. 'You're talking about relationships and *entitlement* in the same breath? Relationships are about sharing and caring and being equal—you wouldn't know one if it came up and hit you in the face! In fact, for all your power and wealth and achievements, you really don't have a clue about life, do you, Salvatore? In fact, you're more of a robot than a man!'

'You think so?' It was an insult too far and the anger which had been bubbling away inside him suddenly transmuted into something much more manageable. His arm went out to pull her up against his hips and to press her hard against him. 'Want me to show you how much of a man I am?'

The arrogant boast should have repelled her, but it did no such thing—emotions and temper were running so high that it was like putting a match to a bone-dry timber. He was hot and he was hard. And heaven help her but Jessica's body responded to him with an overpowering greed—even while her mind and her heart battled against his powerful influence. 'No,' she breathed, when—maddeningly—he loosened his grip on her.

Correctly, he read the disappointment which clouded her grey eyes and gave a soft laugh. 'That would drive your point home, wouldn't it, Jessica *mia*? The big, bad wolf who just takes his pleasure when and where he wants it.' He lifted her chin with his finger. 'But you want it, too, don't you?'

Her eyelids fluttered down.

'Yes, you want me badly. You always did and you always will.' And he wanted her, too. Still. His discovery about her lies and duplicity were the perfect get-out clause—giving him the freedom to walk away from her now without a pang. Without all the tears and scenes he had anticipated.

But he didn't want to.

Not yet.

Not until the inexplicable fever she evoked in his blood had vanished once and for all.

'Jessica,' he said softly, and brushed his lips against hers.

The sudden change of mood took her off guard—the soft kiss hinting at a tenderness she secretly longed for. And he knew that. He knew her weak spots. He knew what women wanted because he was a clever man who'd had women throwing themselves at him ever since he'd grown out of short trousers. He's playing with you, she told herself—playing exactly as a cat plays with a mouse before it lures the innocent little creature towards its horrible fate.

So stop him. She wriggled a little—but that had precisely the wrong effect.

'Don't fight me for the sake of fighting me,' he murmured against her mouth. 'Not when you want this just as much as I do.'

And in a way, his cruel perception only heightened her hunger. She had shown herself to be a liar. She had sold his costly gift in secret and, no matter how worthy the cause, didn't that make her look cheap? Nothing would ever redeem her in his eyes and so she had nothing to lose. Nothing.

'Who's fighting?' she questioned throatily, beginning to unbutton his shirt.

Her instant compliance was less surprising than the fact that she had taken the initiative and was slipping the silk from his shoulders. And now she was unbuckling his belt…pulling at it impatiently and sliding down the zip. He choked as she slipped her hand inside, circling him with possessive eroticism as she began to stroke him.

'Jessica!' He choked out her name on a shuddering entreaty, but she calmly finished undressing him and then pushed him to the ground with an authority which was a breathtaking turn-on to watch.

Barely able to breathe for excitement, he watched as she peeled off her dress with a fluid movement and tossed it aside. And now all she was wearing was a frothy concoction of black lace bra and panties with stockings and a suspender belt. His tongue snaked out to moisten a mouth which felt like parchment as she slithered out of the panties and they joined the discarded dress on the floor, and he could see exactly what she was going to do. Exactly. To lower herself down on top of him and to…to…

'*Dio*, Jessica!' he gasped as she straddled him and pleasure surged through him like a high-voltage shock. But that was exactly what it was. She was the sweetest and most teachable lover a man could ever ask for—but usually she bowed to *his* experience and *he* was the one who always took the lead. Yet not this time. Oh, not this time. 'What are you doing?' he gasped.

'Don't you know?' she queried mock-innocently as she moved her hips—and yet she wasn't quite sure herself. All she knew was that he could turn on her with a speed which drove home just how temporary her place in his life really was. So why not give him the kind of treatment he clearly wanted? Why not play the accomplished mistress and leave him with the memory of *this*? She moved again.

'*Donna seducente*!' he moaned.

'What does that mean?'

'Witch!'

'Am I?'

'*Sì*. Ah, *sì*!'

At least the compliment showed that her seduction was working even if it didn't sound like the Jessica she really was—whose heart had been lost to this emotionless Sicilian. It made her sound like a real temptress of a woman, a woman totally comfortable in her own skin who knew how to please her man. But for a moment that was exactly what she felt like—even if the image was simply an illusion, because Salvatore was not *her* man, and he never would be.

She kept her eyes closed as she rode him, not wanting to see his expression for fear of what it would tell her and not daring to let him see what was in hers.

Because he doesn't want your love.

He groaned again as she increased the pace. This was all he wanted, she reminded herself. This, and this, and…

'Jessica!' Her name was wrenched from his lips and she opened her eyes just as the first blissful spasms began to catch hold of her too, and their eyes met in a naked moment of pure pleasure.

'Jessica,' he said again as he shuddered within her, lost in her spell and deep within her body.

Afterwards, she sank down onto his chest as his arms came up to enfold her. And in the aftermath of spent passion it was all too easy to forget what had led to that moment. The bitter words and the recriminations. The realisation of how temporary this all was and her growing recognition of just how badly it was going to hurt once it was over. Jessica screwed her eyes tightly shut to hold the tears at bay. She wanted to hold onto this moment for ever. This man.

'Jessica?'

His voice was sleepy but Jessica didn't underestimate him, not for a minute. He was a master of timing, after all—and the end might come when she was least expecting it. When she was warm and sated in his embrace. Was he going to tell her now? Well, she would be calm and dignified. She'd known what was going to happen when she walked into this—so she could hardly turn round and weep when it did. And yet already she could feel the sharp ache in her heart as she imagined a life without him.

'Yes, Salvatore?'

He caught hold of her hips and deftly turned her onto her back and then rolled on top of her, his blue eyes glittering and hard as they gazed down at her.

'Don't ever lie to me again,' he said softly.

Jessica blinked up at him. She had been mentally preparing herself for the inevitable and now she stared at him, feeling lost and wrong-footed. 'But I thought...' Her voice tailed off in confusion.

'What did you think, *cara mia*? That I would be unable to forgive you?'

The taste of fear felt bitter in her mouth. 'Well, yes.'

He enjoyed her confusion; savoured it. 'On the contrary—I forgive you. Everyone deserves a second chance, my beauty.' Stroking his fingertips over the delicate lace of the bra she had not bothered to remove, he felt her tremble and he gave a hard-edged smile. 'And that was far too good a performance for me not to want to repeat it.'

Performance? 'Is that supposed to be a compliment?' she questioned shakily.

'It's the truth,' he said roughly. 'Now let's go to bed and you can do it all over again.'

CHAPTER FOURTEEN

BUT Jessica soon realised that Salvatore's idea of 'forgiveness' wasn't the same as hers. Not at all. He might have decided it wasn't worth ending their relationship because she'd sold the bracelet and then lied about it—but that didn't make everything magically better between them. How could it? Something had changed—and that something was his attitude towards her.

Before she had felt as though she was getting occasional glimpses at the chinks in his armour. As if he sometimes allowed her to see the living and breathing man beneath the hard exterior—and every time he did it had felt like a little victory. But not any more.

Was it because he no longer trusted her that the shutters had come banging down and now seemed to completely exclude her? That the ease and relaxation she had started to feel in his company had disappeared, to be replaced with an inner ice she could no longer penetrate, nor even dare to. And that while the sex was as good as it had ever been, it was as if he now took a calculated pleasure in demonstrating every skill in his sensual repertoire. Almost as if he wanted to taunt her with it.

Did he mean to make her heart ache? she wondered. During those moments of intimacy, did he intend her to imagine the terrible gap he would leave in her life when he was gone? Because she was getting very good at that.

That carefree weekend in Paris now seemed as if it had happened to another couple. She even found herself longing for those simple days when she'd cleaned his office, when he used to confide in her and ask her advice—sometimes even listen to it. That was *true* intimacy, she thought wistfully. Much more than wearing the fine clothes he bought for her and then having him strip them from her body.

The telephone rang and Jessica jumped as she picked it up, even though she had been waiting for him to ring for the past hour. These days she felt as if her whole life was a waiting game. Some nights he booked ahead with her—especially if it was for some grand dinner, or opera. But others—like tonight—were dependent on Salvatore's mood and how long his meetings ran for.

'Hello,' she said in a strained voice.

'Jessica?'

'Hello, Salvatore.' Pulling herself together, she forced herself to sound interested, to rid herself of the succession of doubts which were spinning around in her head like a washing machine. 'How…how was your meeting?'

'Tedious—I don't really want to talk about it.' He stifled a yawn. 'Can you be ready to go out to dinner in an hour?'

Jessica frowned into the mirror. It would need a small

miracle to get her presentable enough for his exacting eyes in that time. 'But I thought you said you wanted a quiet evening in.'

'Did I? Sorry—change of plan. A friend of mine is unexpectedly in town with his girlfriend and wants to meet up. I thought she'd like a little female company.'

What could she say? That she was delighted to meet his friends? Because it didn't feel like that. It was less of an invitation and more of a command—but Jessica would be there because that was her role. To be available. To be ready whenever her lover snapped his fingers. To mould herself to *his* desires.

'Sure I can,' she said, hating herself for her weakness.

He sent a car to collect her, and when Jessica walked into the restaurant Salvatore was already seated with the guests and rose to his feet to greet her. And, as always, her heart turned over when she saw his dark and imposing figure.

'Ciao,' said Salvatore softly as he kissed her on each cheek—the swift, sleek movement of his hand over her hip an indication of what she might expect from him later. 'Meet Giovanni and Maria,' he added. 'This is Jessica.'

'Hello,' said Jessica, wondering what he'd actually told them about her.

Giovanni Amato was a rather daunting and powerful Sicilian and his girlfriend was very sweet, but the three of them kept lapsing into Italian. And even though they switched to English when they realised they were doing it, it only increased Jessica's bubbling feeling of insecurity.

She felt like an alien, an outsider. Staring at the congealing red-wine sauce on her plate, she found herself wondering what the hell she was doing here. At least Giovanni and Maria seemed like a *real* couple, while she felt as disposable as the crumbs from the bread rolls which the waiter was disposing of with a tiny brush.

You're nothing to Salvatore, she thought painfully as she watched his dark and beautiful profile laughing at something Giovanni had just said. Nothing solid or enduring. You're just here to even up the numbers and to satisfy his overwhelming sexual hunger when the evening is over.

And you care for him far more than he will ever care for you.

She said little in the car on the way to his Chelsea home and Salvatore shot her a glance as she stared out at the passing streets. He thought how pensive and pale she looked. And why was that? he wondered. 'You're very quiet tonight, cara,' he observed silkily.

She turned her head. 'Am I?'

He lifted her hand—beautifully manicured and showing none of the roughness of her cleaning days. Was she quiet for a reason? Perhaps it was time to sweeten her up with a gift. Another piece of jewellery, maybe. His mouth hardened. Or maybe he should just give her cash—at least that would save her the trouble of selling it and cut out the middleman!

'You know you are. Maybe you're tired,' he observed, a question in his voice as he lifted her fingertips to his lips, kissing each one in turn.

'Not a bit of it,' said Jessica brightly as she stared into the glittering black coldness of his eyes. Because mistresses weren't supposed to be tired, were they? They had to be pampered and preened and gleaming and sheening and stripped ready for action whenever their lover wanted them to be.

But as the car slid to a powerful halt in front of Salvatore's apartment, Jessica knew that she couldn't carry on with this. Not any more. Her self-respect and her self-worth were being whittled away with every second she remained as his mistress.

It had been wrong from the start and time was only making that more apparent. Maybe the whole diamond bracelet incident had just brought it to a head sooner. And if she didn't get out now, then she was going to suffer unbearable heartbreak. She needed to get out while she still had a choice to recover. She needed to tell him.

But not until the morning. Just one more night of bliss in his arms—surely that wasn't too much to ask for?

Once inside his apartment, she turned to him—suddenly realising just how much she was going to miss him.

'Salvatore,' she whispered, her lips brushing against the hard line of his jaw as she began to unknot his silk tie.

He looked down at her. 'What is it, *tranquilo cara*?'

Knowing that this was to be the last time made her want to reach out to him in a way she knew she never could. So reach out to him in the only way you can. The only way he'll let you. She stared up at him. 'I want...to go to bed.'

'Oh, do you?' He could feel the sudden breathless urgency in her trembling body and, as always, a heady response surged fiercely through his own. 'So do I,' he said unsteadily.

In a way, it was both the best and the worst kind of farewell. It was Salvatore as she would always remember him—at his most tender and passionate throughout the night. But it's just sex, she told herself. And men can do that—particularly men like Salvatore. They can make it seem as though it means something, when it doesn't. Not a thing.

She slept fitfully and, waking early, showered and dressed before collecting her few bits and pieces from the bathroom. Apart from a couple of spare pairs of panties which were stuffed into Salvatore's sock drawer, that was pretty much all she had to show from her time there.

When she came through to the kitchen, Salvatore was also up and dressed, drinking coffee and reading through a sheaf of papers. Automatically, he poured her a cup and pushed it towards her. The smell was tantalising and she gave him a weak smile of thanks. How domesticity could mock you with its false intimacy, she thought, and her heart gave a painful lurch at the thought of what she had to do.

She took the coffee but her fingers were trembling too much for her to dare pick it up and instead she looked up at him, trying not to be affected by the dark, tousled beauty of his face—but it wasn't easy. 'Salvatore, I want to talk to you.'

'Can't it wait?' His fingers flicked over the bundle

of legal documents. 'I have meetings all day and want to read through these first.'

She swallowed, but shook her head. 'No, I'm afraid it can't wait.'

A flicker of impatience crossed his face, but then it was gone. He sighed. 'What is it, Jessica?'

'I just wanted you to know that I'm not...' She ran her tongue over her lips. 'That I shan't be seeing you any more.'

For a moment he thought he might have misheard her, but the uptight expression on her face told him otherwise. He didn't react. 'Go on,' he said softly.

'And I just wanted to say that I've enjoyed—well, if not quite *every* second of being your mistress, then most of it. Definitely.'

Salvatore put his papers down on the breakfast bar. 'And that's it?'

She nodded. 'That's it.'

'Do you want to tell me why?'

It was a measure of the inequality of their relationship that Jessica was almost flattered that he was bothered enough to ask! But she suspected that a man who was so suspicious of feelings and wary of commitment wouldn't really want to know all the nuts and bolts which had brought her to her decision. Would he care if she told him that she felt like an object, that she was in love with him and that she feared her heart would break if she let it just drift on and on until he ended it? No, of course he wouldn't.

Jessica paused. 'I just think our relationship has run its course.'

There was a long, tense silence before his words sliced through it. 'It won't work, you know.' He spoke with silken threat as he met her eyes with a look of pure blue steel. Didn't she realise that *he* was the one who always ended the relationship? That *he* was the one in control?

'What won't?' she whispered.

'If this ridiculous *gesture* of yours is some kind of ultimatum trying to get me to commit to you, Jessica—to get a damned ring on your finger—then I can assure you that you're wasting your time! It's been tried before and it hasn't worked and it won't work this time. I don't bow to pressure—either in the boardroom nor the bedroom; I never have.'

She stared at him in horror. 'It is not a *gesture*, Salvatore!' she returned. 'It's real! And neither is it an ultimatum. It's something I've been thinking about for some time and your reaction is making me question why on earth it took me so long.'

He rose from his seat and approached her with a look on his face that she had never seen there before. Dark and smouldering with anger—with all the slow-burn intensity of a carefully banked fire.

'I shan't change my mind, you know,' he said softly.

'I'm not expecting you to,' she blustered. 'I don't...*want* you to.'

At this he stilled and an odd kind of smile twisted his lips into a cruel and mocking smile. 'Oh, you don't?'

'No.' She should have seen it coming, but she didn't realise what he was going to do until she felt the hard, warm impact of his body. And then she knew he was going to kiss her—and she knew exactly why and it made her shudder. Because this had nothing to do with affection. It was a branding, a stamp—a mark of indelible possession—intended to spoil her for every other man who followed him.

And how bizarre that even while the Jessica who had just finished the affair should dread that kiss—the Jessica who loved him longed for it more than anything else in the world.

His lips were hard and hungry. If sexual excellence could be demonstrated in one brief and utterly arousing display, then Salvatore Cardini should have taken out a patent on that kiss.

It left her reeling and gasping for breath, even after he dropped his hands from her body and turned to walk out of the room. Just by the door he stopped to turn his head and look at her. And suddenly this was not the Salvatore she knew, but the face of a dark and forbidding stranger with icy blue eyes.

'Make sure you clear all your stuff out of here,' he said, with icy precision. 'And leave your key behind when you go.'

Somehow she managed not to react during the time it took him to grab his stuff and to slam the front door behind him. It was after that, of course, that the tears came, without mercy.

CHAPTER FIFTEEN

THE typewritten words danced in a meaningless haze on the page and Salvatore's lips curled.

He should have been a happy man.

Liberated from a relationship which had begun to look tricky. Freed from a low-class little gold-digger who had foolishly overestimated her power over him. The London side of the business was enjoying a record year under his stewardship and his social calendar was as busy as he wished it to be. Yes, he should have been, not merely happy, but *ecstatic*.

So what was it that troubled him? Which made him restless, unable to settle? Which had him remembering those wide grey eyes and pink-petal lips and shiny hair spread all over his pillow? The way her skin felt so soft when he drifted his lips to her neck.

Damn her!

Viciously, he jabbed the nib of his pen into the tail end of a signature and pushed the signed pile of letters towards his secretary, ignoring her perplexed expression. He knew that his mood had been black and that he had been bringing it with him to the office and yet he couldn't quite seem to stop himself—and neither could he pinpoint the exact cause for his discontentment. For a man used to having all the solutions at his fingertips, it was an unwelcome and unusual state of affairs.

Was it because Jessica had been the one who had finished the relationship—was that it? He stared out of the window. Very probably—since he was the one who liked to dominate and control. Maybe it was because such an action had wounded his pride—and to a Sicilian, pride was everything. Salvatore's mouth hardened.

And maybe most of all it was because he still wanted to have sex with her—because the strange, sensual magic she had woven over his body had not yet been exorcised.

So what was he going to do about it?

Leaning back in his chair, he ran a thoughtful thumb over the dark rasp of new growth at his jaw. The answer, it seemed, was ridiculously easy.

Why not get her back into his bed for one night—to remind her just what she'd been missing? He felt the hard curl of lust at his groin. And to remind himself what he'd been missing, too. Salvatore ran his tongue over his lips. To have her sob out her fulfilment once more in his arms as she lay beneath him...wouldn't that help purge her from his system once and for all? Meaning that he could walk away and finally forget all about her?

He lifted the phone and punched out her number, surprised at the wariness he heard in her voice when she answered. His ex-lovers usually gushed like oil wells if he deigned to speak to them, instead of speaking in small, clipped tones like these. Surely she should have sounded a little more *grateful* to hear from him again than that?

Once they had swopped meaningless little pleasantries, she came straight to the point.

'What can I do for you, Salvatore?'

Fractionally, he elevated his brows. Why, for a moment there, she had made it sound almost as if he were disturbing her! 'Remember that trip we'd planned to the opera on the fifteenth?' he purred. 'Well, you were looking forward to it so much that I've decided we should still go.'

In the Shepherd's Bush house, Jessica stared at her paper-pale face in the mirror, trembling with rage as she marvelled at his arrogant assumption. Because concentrating on that was better than allowing herself to focus on how badly she missed him, how much her heart ached just to hear his voice.

'I can't do that,' she said.

'Why not?'

She wanted to ask him if he was insane. Didn't he have any idea of how painful it was to be apart from him—despite the fact that she kept telling herself over and over again that he was an egotistical tyrant? No, of course he didn't. Acknowledging that would require a little insight and tenderness and genuine emotion—and Salvatore didn't do any of *those* things.

'Because it's not appropriate,' she said slowly. 'Since we are no longer a couple.'

For a moment he thought that she must be playing games, teasing him by putting on a show of reluctance before agreeing to go with him—since they both knew that was what she wanted. But nothing but silence followed her remark.

'You *are* joking?'

'No, Salvatore, I'm not.'

He found himself in the unheard of position of trying to *persuade* a woman to go out with him! 'But it's a world-famous production of one of the most moving operas of all time.'

'Nobody's denying that.'

'And you were desperate to see it.'

Not *that* desperate. 'I'm sure you can find someone else to go with you,' she said.

'And you'd be happy with that?' he demanded. 'Me taking another woman?'

'My feelings on your choice of date are irrelevant.'

'Well, I suggest you think about it,' he said silkily. 'And then let me know.'

But to Salvatore's astonishment—she didn't! There was no phone-call or text. No email or unannounced visit—telling him that she had been a little too hasty and that of course she would love to accompany him to the opera.

Undaunted—indeed, a little fired up by the unexpected chase—Salvatore ordered a gown to be sent to her home, along with a diamond necklace, which was bound to tempt her. Then he sat back and waited for her phone-call.

It wasn't what he had been expecting. Why, she sounded almost *angry*.

'Salvatore—why have you sent these gifts?'

'You don't like them?'

Jessica stared down at the scarlet dress. It was the colour of a poppy, made from the softest silk imaginable and so utterly exquisite that she did not dare try it. The diamond necklace was even more dazzling—pear-shaped drops of rainbow ice dangled in a brilliant loop, falling through her fingers in a glittering stream of light. She swallowed. Did he think she could be bought by such ostentatious presents? 'Why?' she repeated.

Oh, but she was playing with fire. She knew *exactly* why he had sent them. 'They are a sweetener, *cara,*' he purred. 'Wear them to the opera. You'll look wonderful wearing them.'

Of course she wanted to wear them—but she liked them because *he* had sent them and not because of what they were worth. Just as she longed to see *him* and not the wretched opera. But she did not dare—how could she risk her emotional security by putting herself back in a vulnerable situation with a man who didn't love her?

Praying for courage, Jessica closed her fingers over the gems, blocking out their brilliance. 'Let me say it again, Salvatore—I'm not coming to the opera with you.'

Furiously, Salvatore drummed his fingers against one tensed thigh. 'What does it take to persuade you, Jessica?' he demanded. 'You want emeralds? Or a rock the size of Gibraltar?'

He still didn't get it, did he? 'I cannot be *bought*!' she stormed. 'I am *not* for sale!'

It was the first time a woman had ever hung up on

him and Salvatore found himself staring at the disconnected phone with an air of mystification. She had slammed the phone down on him!

He went to his club and swam before having dinner with a wealthy sheikh, but all the time his mind kept drifting back to Jessica and the fiery determination he had heard in her voice.

Did she mean what she said? It seemed that perhaps she did.

Bizarrely, he found time suddenly empty on his hands with nothing but troubled thoughts to fill it. He found himself remembering that weekend in Paris—before he'd discovered that she'd sold the bracelet. It had been about as perfect a weekend as he could have imagined—and yet he remembered, too, the near-joy with which he had leapt on her deception. He had *wanted* to think badly of her.

But she'd sold the jewels to care for her grandmother, hadn't she? He knew that. So did that make her a bad person, or a caring person?

He frowned. And there was something else, too—something which nudged at the edges of his memory.

On the advice of his secretary, he spent the afternoon in Camden market—a busy, hippy sort of place, not his usual kind of destination at all. And he wasn't really sure what he was looking for until he found it.

Later that evening, he knocked on the door of Jessica's house in Shepherd's Bush and the tall girl who was named after the tree opened the door to him, her eyes opening wide in surprise when she saw him, her hand going up immediately to smooth down her tousled blonde hair.

'Oh, hello!'

'I'm looking for Jessica,' he said.

Her face fell. 'I'll go and tell her.'

He could hear the sound of muffled voices and his mouth twisted. If Jessica thought that she was going to get away with not seeing him, then she was wrong. He would kick the damned door down first. And then suddenly she was standing in front of him, looking small—almost frail—in a pair of old, faded jeans and an equally faded sweater.

'Hello, Salvatore,' she said quietly. 'What…what do you want?'

Her face was pale, her grey eyes huge and she was staring up at him with a solemn expression on her face. It was the least welcoming look he could have imagined and Salvatore's eyes narrowed.

'May I come in?'

She wanted to say no, to slam the door in his face. And yet she wanted to gather him in and pull him close against the body which had yearned for him since the last time she had held him.

But her face registered none of this. 'Of course,' she said politely.

He was ushered into the same rather drab sitting room he remembered from a previous visit and Jessica stood looking at him expectantly.

'What can I do for you, Salvatore?'

He recognised that there was to be no warm and

unquestioning welcome and that too surprised him. And apologies didn't come easy to a man who had rarely had to make them. 'I realise that I have offended you,' he began.

She wondered which particular incident he had in mind, but she said nothing.

'That sending you the diamonds and the dress was a rather inelegant gesture.' He gave a short laugh. 'Even though you are probably the only woman in the world who would think so.' Awkwardly, he pulled a slim box from his pocket and handed it to her. 'So I want you to have this instead.'

She stood there, just staring at it. *Still* he didn't get it, did he? 'I don't want it.'

'Take it. Please.'

Something in the way he asked her made it impossible for her to refuse. Reluctantly, Jessica took the box from him and snapped open the lid. Yet it was not the glitter of priceless jewels which greeted her—but an oval moonstone which lay at the centre of a simple silver chain. It was milky-grey—with a kind of inner radiance—the colour of a river. It stirred a memory, but more than that—it stirred her heart.

Stupidly, she felt a lump rise to her throat, the salty flicker of tears at the backs of her eyes, but she blinked them away because it didn't *mean* anything. It was just another offering—another object—a currency with which Salvatore was attempting to buy her.

'I remember you said you liked moonstones,' said Salvatore, and in that moment he felt like the insecure teenager he had never had to be. 'That they reminded you of the Seine.'

For a moment she couldn't speak as she stared down at them. Just nodded. 'Yes. They…they do.' She looked up at him. 'But why have you bought it?'

Salvatore's features hardened. Surely she knew that! 'Because I want to end this stand-off,' he growled. 'I want you back in my life.'

Jessica studied the face which she loved in spite of everything. The beginning of a smile had begun to curve his beautiful lips—because Salvatore would not have considered for a moment that her answer might be anything other than the one he wanted to hear.

And, oh, how easy it would be to have just said yes. To have fallen into his arms with the foolish hopes which her stupid heart couldn't quite keep at bay. But what was the point? She would only be opening up the floodgates to more pain and more heartache. Let their affair stay exactly how it was—slowly dying and fading away to become nothing more than a bittersweet memory.

She shook her head. 'I can't,' she whispered. 'I just can't.'

He seized on the word, ready to do battle with it. 'Can't?'

'I'm not prepared to carry on being your mistress, Salvatore. I just can't do it any more.'

He stared at her. 'Why not?'

Did he want her to spell it out in order to try to win her round with words, or kisses? Or because he simply didn't understand? And maybe he didn't. Maybe

Salvatore had spent his whole life with women giving him exactly what *he* wanted—so that it simply might not have occurred to him that women had needs, too.

'Because the affair has run its course,' she managed. 'It's past its sell-by date. It no longer feels like fun. It feels grubby. Temporary. And I'm not prepared to carry on being your mistress any more.' Painfully, she shrugged her shoulders. 'I've outgrown my role in your life, Salvatore—and you need to find a replacement.'

But as he looked at her bright eyes and trembling lips, something was happening to him—a sudden overwhelming feeling which crystallised into a bone-sure certainty that he didn't *want* a replacement. And that here was a woman who made his heart and his blood sing. Who was making him fight for her. A woman worth fighting for. So fight, Cardini. *Fight!*

'But nobody can replace you, Jessica,' he said urgently. 'No other woman makes me feel the way you do. You feel so right in my life—you always did—and nothing seems the same without you.' He could see her petalled lips begin to open—maybe to mouth her objections—and he shook his head. 'I know you don't want to be my mistress any more—but I don't want you to be. I realise that you do not care for the things my money can buy—that I have gone about this like a fool. A novice.' Now he shrugged, holding the palms of his hands open in a gesture which was almost helpless. 'But then I *am* a novice,' he breathed. 'You see, I have never been in love before, Jessica. My heart is full of love, *cara mia*—and I want you to marry me. That is—'

and his blue eyes glittered with a touch of his familiar arrogance '—if you love me, too.'

There was a breathless pause. 'You know I do,' she whispered.

Their eyes met in a long moment as he held his arms out. 'Ah, Jessica,' he said tenderly. 'Come to me.'

Jessica thought she must be crying, but things were such a blur because she seemed to be laughing, too—with disbelief and joy and wonder—as she went to him like a homing pigeon.

And he gathered her close against his body, stroking the silk of her hair. 'Believe that I love you,' he whispered, just before he kissed her. 'And now let me show you just how much.'

EPILOGUE

'AND your grandmother is happy, I think?'

Beneath the warmth of the Sicilian sun, Jessica smiled at Salvatore as they stood watching the family party, which showed no signs of finishing. It was his nephew Gino's third birthday and the noise levels had been steadily increasing all afternoon, but soon the cake would be cut and then things might start to calm down!

All the different generations of Cardinis were playing some complicated Sicilian version of the game 'catch' and her grandmother seemed to have a natural aptitude for the game, which was making her opponents crow with disbelief.

Jessica wrapped her arms around Salvatore's waist, her heart so full of happiness that she felt it might burst. 'Oh, *caro*—she just loves it. Yet I never thought she'd leave England!'

Salvatore's mouth curved. 'For Sicily? And who in their right mind would turn down an opportunity to live in a place such as this?'

Who indeed? How perfect life had become—so

perfect that sometimes Jessica felt as if she would soon wake up. But this was no dream; this was her reality.

Salvatore had made her his wife in a simple service in a beautiful church in Trapani. The choir's voices had soared in that cool and sacred place, filled with the fragrance of the same white flowers which had been wreathed in abundance around her veil.

When he'd first asked her to marry him and move to his homeland, Jessica had told him that she felt bad about leaving her grandmother in England. 'I mean, I know Sicily's only a plane journey away, but even so I'm the only family she's got, and—'

'But your grandmother will come with us,' he had said, as if no other possibility would ever be entertained. 'In Sicily, family is everything—and every member has their valued place in it.'

Especially wives, it seemed, thought Jessica—still glowing from the passion and the tenderness with which he had woken her this morning. For a man who had fought shy of expressing love, Salvatore certainly seemed to be making up for it!

The Cardini complex was enormous—and the family owned properties on all sides of the island. There was room enough for everyone to mingle without overlapping too much. Because space was important, too. And her grandmother had already formed a deep and close bond with young Gino, which was probably a good thing, as his English mother Emma had confided to Jessica—since she was expecting a second baby.

Salvatore had dissuaded his hot-headed cousin

Giacomo from buying the Phuket hotel and had instead offered him the job of replacing him as chairman in London, since he had decided to relocate to Sicily with his new bride.

And Jessica was learning Italian—or rather, she was learning to speak Sicilian since, as everyone told her rather sternly, the two were really very different.

In fact, on this earthly paradise with Salvatore by her side, she was learning so much about everything that was important. But mostly about love.

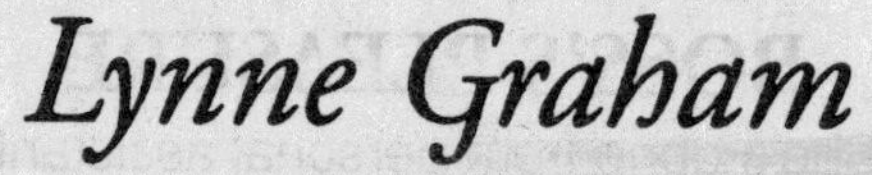

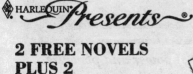

I
HARLEQUIN®
Presents